DISBANDED KINGDOM

DISBANDED KINGDOM

POLIS LOIZOU

First published in the United Kingdom in 2018
by Cloud Lodge Books (CLB)

A CIP catalogue record for this book is available from the British Library.

ISBN 978-0-9954657-9-4

1 3 5 7 9 10 8 6 4 2

01 MUSK

Maybe God is the man he needs.

Midnight's been and gone, left him stranded in a part of the city his feet have never tramped before. An odour with a tang, like the remaining salt in a tub of popcorn, hangs between the blocks of flats. Then there's the scent of the man himself, tossed back and laid out to guide him, a leather road through the dark. It's a shaky need taking hold of Oscar, for the stranger to turn around and notice him. One look, then the guy can carry on walking.

The noise of boys ricochets around the streets. A droning rap and a dancehall rhythm, pumping from about the wheels. It comes back to him, that story glimpsed in strangers' Metros on the tube. A man got stabbed to death in Croydon, waiting for a bus with his kid. Same could go for him tonight — could be scraped off the curb tomorrow with the dog turds and phone-cards for Zimbabwe. The thought propels him along.

The stranger's legs vanish down a side street. They blinked grey in the streetlight and then they were gone. It was those legs that spurred Oscar on in the first place. Caught his eye in Caffè Nero, when the man stood up in his sharp grey suit, tailored to fit, and dragged his eye further up it 'til Oscar was in Heaven. All other noise in the place had ebbed. That loungy cover of *Nobody's Fault but Mine* coming out of the speakers, sung by some chick far from Nina. Woman sang like she was hosting a suburban barbecue, not mourning her soul in a Baptist church. (Water and fire — faith is elemental, essential.) Back in the café, the man in the grey suit looked to his left, his lime eye trapping the sun. Cut Oscar's breath in half. The guy was hunting, or angry, or horny. Man on a mission. And when he stepped out of the place, Oscar was three steps behind him.

But that was hours ago. The sun has set, the streets have emptied. The stranger's gone from coffee alone to beer in a pub with friends, and somewhere along the way there was the Central line. Bodies pressed together in the rush-hour clash, a guy with sweat patches in Oscar's face and a stout woman with fake nails clipping her iPad. A Nigerian voice in the platform speakers, *Do not obstruct the doors*. There was Charing Cross Road, people with placards decrying something, Tories or terrorists, then Chandos Place and then the Strand, and an old woman with a shawl playing Strauss on a violin as pedestrians passed by. A strand of her hair caught in the breeze, or maybe it was gelled, or so filthy it stood starched and erect in the night.

Now they're in the post-midnight streets, a far cry from Kensington. Far from Charlotte.

She'll be in bed already. She'll've checked her watch and turned in. Straightened his duvet and patted it down in lieu of his thigh. The thought of Charlotte, of going back home to her, makes his stomach go cold. It's not as if anything has happened, other than they forgot how to talk to each other. It used to be easy to play Mother and Son, now it's an endurance test. The time has come to fly the nest.

Grey-suited man has turned a corner. He's been prowling all night, an old-world lycanthrope. The Wolf-Man. Leather shoes on his feet, pointed at the ends and pricking the air. Sharp white teeth, flashed once when he answered his phone on the Strand (the noise of buses drowned his voice out). If only Oscar could touch, and be touched, by this body that won't even glance behind it. There was a moment at the pub earlier, one of those joints made of polished wood and stained glass, where the man turned to his friends and looked in Oscar's direction. The only time he looked at the boy, and didn't even see him. Guys used to, before whatever lever was pulled and their dicks fell limp.

Should've landed a daddy when he had his pick of them. Too late now. The sell-by date sailed by without his even noticing it.

Wolf-Man stood up from his table of buddies. He was going to come over, to flash a grin, punch him, have his way.

Instead, he took his grey-suited self over to the bar to buy another round. His jacket was off, a waistcoat hugged his back. Man was a moving statue, put him on the fourth plinth. Not like his Cityboy buddies back at the table, swigging beers as their shirts cradled man-boobs and bunched at the shoulders.

Wolf-Man's the sort of man who'll turn his back and walk away.

Walk away.

Walk away.

What time is it? What day? The Cityboy friends were wearing pink, so it must be a Friday. Or it was, in any case. Saturday's crept up on them, wherever they are.

No text from Charlotte. She'll imagine he's out with friends, Chelsea girls, sipping bubbly in the backs of cars.

The man's strutting along, who knows where or to whom. Some wench with a beauty vlog, probably. A stylish young bitch in a scarf who'd take it standing up. It makes him cringe. Feminists would slap him, Bella would slap him. But it's too late. The lust has taken hold, parted Oscar from his mind. A man has got into his head again, an untouchable, and he's stepping out of his sharp grey suit.

He's everything Terry wasn't. Pecs like seat cushions, thick hairy arms. He'll wear plain black shorts beneath the trousers, not those ironic-pop-art trunks from H&M. He could grow a full beard if he wanted to. His socks are a single colour and they match. His lips are full. He knows you want him. He doesn't like Shoreditch and he's never heard of Mumford & Sons. He'll never write you a song and he'll never kiss your cheek on the tube. He knows what he's looking for.

When Oscar's thoughts turn to Terry, the boy is always cool in a cloud of smoke, on a red leather sofa. He stares at Oscar, like that first time, and he smiles as he sips his G&T. *Mother's Ruin*. Then they're walking along South Bank, hand-in-hand, weaving their way through the crowds and marvelling at the German Christmas markets. The chocolate-covered fruit and coils of bratwurst. Beer in the air, grilled meat. Terry's black-and-white scarf. His surprisingly deep voice, like a late-night DJ's. That voice hardening as he stands with a taut back across the room, packing his bags and laying their romance to rest.

Unreal as it sometimes seems, it happened. It was, and then it wasn't.

There's nothing in Oscar's room to remind him of Terry now. All that remained were the parting gifts of Bella, Maya and Lukas, former friends of Terry's who switched allegiance in the split. But each of them holds a dozen memories, flashbacks to that old romance, spring-loaded to attack at any given moment. Filmstrips loop in Oscar's head. They play and repeat, and cut, and pause.

Terry in a cloud of smoke on a red leather sofa, smiling as he sips his G&T.

Terry on a red leather sofa.

Terry and his G&T.

A dull ache grinds its way around Oscar's sternum, feels like a spiral or an opening hand. This must be what a tapeworm is like, slithering through your body, munching you skinny as a cokehead model. Or maybe the hunger's more basic. Maybe he should stop at a Subway.

Something in the air says the Thames is nearby, but surely they travelled North? Maybe they've ended up in Camden, Islington, Little Venice — somewhere with canals. In any case, a territory untouched by Charlotte's radar. Graffiti on the walls, FUCK THE SYSTEM and YES, as if in conversation. It would scare her.

Oscar's thoughts must have stayed his pace, 'cause Wolf-Man is far ahead now.

A voice is drifting through the maze of dim-lit blocks. His. The Wolf-Man's.

He's on the phone to someone. Oscar's whole body tenses, his every hair stands to attention — the thousands, the millions...

'Yeah, mate, just getting home.'

And with that, the old sadness descends. Wolf-Man's voice is from a different being. It's too high, too London for those teeth, and those arms, those legs. Throwing words like *awesome* and *pissed* around like an undergrad, when he should've had the gruff voice of a fairytale woodcutter. Bark and musk. Terry wins that round.

A car screeches in the distance, makes them both turn around. It'll be a gang, jumpy-edgy boys with knives. Or Charlotte in a cab, come to take him home.

Neither. It's gone. The quiet takes hold once more.

And the man is facing his way.

Everything goes still. Oscar's been caught by those lime eyes. The stranger's face is hidden in shadows, its expression unclear, but he's undoubtedly looking in Oscar's direction. Now's a time to pray, for faith to do some good.

Oscar's heart freezes. His body goes into autopilot, leans against a lamp-post, without his having planned it. A body made of fumes, pigeon shit and discount porn. The filth of the city. It's lucky he looks so down-and-out, faded T-shirt and well-fucked Converse. Lucky that the dye-job has rusted to pastiche. The man will think him a tramp, or a really shit rent boy. He ponders Oscar. He knows. He's going to come over and slap him, rent him, push him into a canal. Instead he turns his back.

Walks away.

Walks away.

Oscar can't follow. It's so much easier to lean against this wall in the dead of night, to feel like a whore rather than to be in love.

02 SPLASH OF BLUE

Two Middle-Eastern chicks sit outside with their shades and headscarves on, blow shisha smoke into the air. A waiter sets down three bowls of dip and a basket of pitta strips, which they barely acknowledge.

Indoors, away from the sunlight, Bella's switched from moaning about fascists to bitching about fundraisers. 'They see you coming, you know they've seen you coming, and yet it's, like, twelve seconds of feigning ignorance until you're close enough for them to switch on.' She'd spit if it didn't repulse her.

Maya scolds her, playfully. Her bracelets and earrings, turquoise set in copper, jangle as she slaps her friend's knee. That jewellery is her own design. A thing she dreamed up and breathed into life.

Bella carries on regardless. 'Hetero white men feeling disadvantaged by equality are a mess beyond our control. Gremlins with clipboards are at least within our limits.'

Lukas laughs —'It's charity, though!'— and his naked knee bumps Oscar's. A jolt.

'Well, what are those charities spending our donations on, hiring gormless twats to jump around us, dancing and singing? Because they're so like-OMG zany. It's phoney. I know they're just drama graduates reeling off a script. Why should I give ten quid a month, of money my unemployed arse isn't earning, to the blinded widows of Burkina fucking Faso?'

Lukas snorts, bubbles in his coffee.

Maya shakes her head. 'You know what, it's true though. I was with Ali the other day in Hyde Park. And it was all like, really pleasant and sunny? You know, just chillin' on the grass, having a chat. Everybody there was just chillin', when this guy… He was literally going around to everyone in the park trying to get donations. I was, like, *Dude*.'

Bella scowls. She rubs antibacterial gel into her hands, covers them with her sleeves. Lukas stretches as he yawns, a huge grin on his face as he tells the girls they're being bitches. The girls protest, the reaction he wanted. This is the type of male he is to them— has been for years, probably since before college. Since before they met Oscar, before Oscar met Terry. Lukas is the kind of manboy who'll tease a girl and push his luck. But he'd never push far enough to snap, and they know that.

The minutes fade away from Oscar, lose themselves in the shisha haze around Lukas. It's as if a party magician's pulling ribbons from his mouth and nostrils in slow-mo. A plane of brown skin above his high-tops. His thighs against Oscar's, pushing his legs so close together it could geld him. Every part of Lukas is casual, from the loose bare shoulders to the drawl of his voice, to the afro that just-kind-of-happened one winter and stayed. He's the sort of guy people wait for. Wait at a party, wait outside a Picturehouse, a bar, in their bedrooms, on Snapchat, at the clinic, in the queue for a club, for his late-coming and the shoes that amble into the room. So much of his skin on show, through vests or shirts unbuttoned to the abs.

A video plays on the plasma screen above them, in which hunky Arab guys dance around a babe with Shakira hips. No way is it the video of the track coming out of the speaker, a heartfelt lament over a Casio keyboard.

Someone, somewhere, has cried over this.

Maya switches the topic to a guy they know called Sammy, got hitched the other day. Bella refuses to believe they're of marrying age already. But she's got Instagram going on her phone, and is typing her congrats on Sammy's uploads. 'Know what?' she says. 'If this was a hundred years ago, Maya and I would be old maids.'

'Good thing it's not a hundred years ago then.'

Lukas adds that if it were, he and Maya would be Bella's servants. Bella raises her eyebrows at him, *Touché*. His naked knee sends shocks through Oscar's clothed one. Someone has caused offence, or is about to. Bella needs to say something about Oscar, bring him into this, keep the conversation away from Us and Them. *And Oscar would've been my chimneysweep*. Something.

She sips her coffee, no intention of opening her mouth for anything more.

Lukas doesn't like her silence. 'You heard from any jobs yet?' he asks.

'Nope,' she says, and doesn't look up.

He tells her to get on with it. He laughs to show he's joking, a mere attempt to lighten the mood. But Bella stares at him, eyes glowing green in the black mascara.

Maya leads the conversation to a safer place. Her hunt for a flat with Ali, the dives they've been shown to suit their budget. Going East from West has been a wake-up call. But this isn't the right topic either. Bella is silent, until the waiter comes back and asks if she'd like another coffee. She says yes, as long as someone reads her future in the cup afterwards. Maya slaps her knee again, bracelets jangling.

The room grows dark. Joss sticks in the windows, where a strip of lacework hangs, give the place a dull buzz. Little wooden boats bearing Turkish words loll around the counters. A stained-glass lampshade, pink and yellow and orange, hangs from one of the alcoves. The sunlight flicks orange diamonds onto Lukas' jaw, emerald dots on his arms. The smoke spreads around them, apple, until it dissolves.

The singer with the Casio keyboard pines through the speakers, her yearnings drowned out by chatter. She'll be a different kind of woman from the wisp-hipped girl on the screen. Maybe she wears a hijab, sparking hate from every angle— too covered up for some, not enough for others. It's in the nature of his snowflake heart to bleed, to want to find this singer and tell her she's OK in his eyes. But nobody asked for a white fucking knight. Stay put, head down, and shut the fuck up. Snowflake.

Bella's calling his name. She's ended up ahead of him, by the canal. Having looked about her, as if a passerby might be able to explain her friend's behaviour, she winds her way back to him. 'Oskovich, what's up?'

There's a basket on the ground. Wicker, filled with pendants. Glass eyes, each of them blue as the Med, with a splash of white paint and a pupil. They're like cartoons. The boy who's selling them got stuck in a pair of neon trainers, so bright they must be a road-safety initiative.

'I thought you were right behind me,' Bella says. 'I was bitching about vegans when I turned to find a startled goth in a basque staring back at me. I don't know which of us was more appalled.'

Her hand is on Oscar's arm. It stays there, for longer than she'd be comfortable with. Bella's a beast that recoils at touch. If hugs can't be avoided she breaks them quickly, only ever kisses the air when she says goodbye to him or Maya. She calls it parody, and everyone else goes along with it.

Neon-shoed salesboy is staring. And he's been staring at Oscar since he clocked him at the corner's turn. It's the same stare he attracted at school, that mix of curiosity, fear and revulsion. Molotov cocktail of ginger and gay.

Bella looks down at the basket full of Eyes. 'Ooh, pretty!' she says.

'What do you think?' His voice came out ragged, surprised them both.

'For real?' she says, with a look as befits the pregnant daughter of a village pastor.

Maybe it is for real. Maybe God is the man he needs. Charlotte would appreciate that. Might even welcome it.

At the thought of his almost-mother, Oscar's senses return. There's the smell of hot food, the distant tang of weed. The rain that fell, out of the blue, only minutes ago. Spanish, spoken at breakneck speed (or maybe it's Greek— no, Camden, Spanish is more likely). The damp slap of sneakers on stone.

Salesboy hands him an Eye on a string and carries on glaring. Bella ties it around Oscar's neck, and the cold blue glass slips down his shirt. Feels hard on his chest. Maybe God comes after a protein shake. It's only when Bella drags him away, about a hundred yards along the canal bank, that a thought occurs to him— which God is this? What religion? What if it requires circumcision?

The panic of that last thought ebbs to a gentler anxiety. What will Charlotte make of it?

Bella, reading his mind, says, 'It's Charlotte's thing tonight, innit?'

'Yeah.'

'You excited? Picked out your best frock?' She's expecting more from him. A couple of phrases to set the scene. The book launch, Bellinis and Boodles. What Charlotte will be wearing, what he'll be dressed in. All that fuss over something so transient. Over the past few months, Bella's come to accept that Oscar's tongue has vanished, out with the red hair dye and the thigh-high boots, only to make a bashful appearance once in a blue moon. The subject is dropped.

A few feet away, there's a stall selling prints. Some hang on boards, some stand freely, all are guarded by a sour merchant. Man has a face like a road sign, a white triangle of teeth showing through his upturned lip. You wanna buy something? He couldn't give a shit. 'What kind of service do you expect,' Bella says, 'from someone who abuses apostrophes?' She licks her finger and rubs a culprit out of the price board, then squirts antibacterial gel on her hands.

There's a Banksy print of Dorothy, basket being searched by police while Toto barks on. That other one, of the masked youth hurling a bunch of flowers like a grenade. Lesser artists' ink drawings of London landmarks. Photos of a couple having sex in a public toilet, poster-size and ready for a fauxhemian studio flat in Dalston. Maya's new flatshare, probably.

Everything is pointless.

Bella flicks through the laminated posters at their legs. Marilyn, Judy, Pacino, DeNiro, Depp, and settles on Brando. 'Screw Bon Jovi, this is what I'm talking about. Is Charlotte ever gonna write about ol' Brando here? I swear, I could write a twenty-thousand-word thesis solely on his vest.'

A montage of *Streetcar Named Desire* scenes fills Oscar's head. An old in-joke returns to him. 'You want to be *nice* to him.'

Bella blinks, startled. Those green eyes in the black mascara. Then she grins. 'I want to be *very* nice to him.'

Satisfied, she takes Oscar by the arm, turns him back in the direction of the high street and the station. She sighs into the evening. 'Camden looks so pretty after the fire.'

She's right, it does look pretty. In the pink-golden light, in the coolness of the air by the canal, the hanging T-shirts, *Star Wars*, Heisenberg, *NOBODY KNOWS I'M A LESBIAN*, the prints and the doughnuts, the bongs, the humping-skeleton ornaments, the zodiac fridge magnets and the skull candle-holders, are all imbued with a wistful beauty.

'Are you alright, Osky?' Bella says, a Murray Mint on her breath.

'Yeah. Why?'

She tilts her head closer, scans his face for the truth. 'Darling, your eyes are rather moist.'

'No, it's…'

She only nods.

Ten feet away, a fight's going down. One guy slams another guy's chest. 'You startin', bruv?!' Others gather 'round, spoiling for a chance. Someone's wandered down the wrong postcode. Bella leads Oscar away. Last thing they need is to witness a stabbing. She takes them to a spot on the canal bank where steaming curries come out of vans in Styrofoam trays. Food you pick at with a plastic fork, astride the back end of a sawn-off motorbike, looking out at the water. Tourists in backpacks occupy the whole row of half-bikes, each of them dining alone. One guy eats like a bear, jaw quaking, stubble about to fall off his chin. Daddy. A cousin of the Wolf-Man from the other night. Wherever he is, whatever he's up to now.

Bella elbows Oscar. 'I want to be nice to him too,' she says, looking at the same guy, and giggles.

Daddy is hot, but in that scary-aloof way. He grimaces at something in his mouth, then spits it out on the ground.

'Oh,' Bella says, 'fuck that, then.' And the romance is shot.

The front door swings open before his hand has even reached for it. Charlotte's eyes stand wide, a small black pupil in a splash of blue. Even in the dim light of her candles, lined up along the carved wooden sideboard, she spotted the Eye with the skill of a sniffer-dog. Dorothy being searched by police.

'Oh, darling!' she says, smiling, and leans forward to kiss his cheek. 'You're ever so late.'

Jo Malone. Mint and jasmine.

She parts their bodies to hold the Eye at his neck. 'Where did you get this?'

'Camden.'

'I haven't been to Camden in decades,' she says with a laugh. 'It's beautiful.'

She means the Eye, its cobalt glass turned indigo in the half-light. The reflected glimmer of the candles on its surface. A current of relief surges through him. Not that she would've yelled at him or locked him in a turret, but there could have arisen a vague resentment, left unspoken, over something like this. Who knows, maybe there has. Emotions lie on top of each other, vocals in counterpoint, different elements mingling into something new. There once was a day when he would've hugged her back.

She pats his shoulder, turns him in the direction of his bedroom and tells him he really ought to change. Carolina has pressed his trousers, and that periwinkle shirt from Liberty. 'I thought it would look best,' she says.

And she's right. It does.

Twenty minutes later, the cab is waiting outside. The corridor is still, as if the whole floor has been put to sleep. On the way down, Charlotte's perfume fills the lift, clogs his head, and when her body turns to the parting of the doors, her exit comes as a swift, cool blow.

The tall white ramparts of Mayfair drift by. Charlotte's face has become a screen for the projected lights of the city, the streetlamps, the shops, the passing buses. Out on the street, a woman's scarlet coat billows as she bends to grab her phone from the pavement. Another woman, nearby, gesticulates at her. You can never get inside another person's head. Seconds later, the cab's pulled up at the gallery, where everyone's inside and waiting. Charlotte overpays the cabbie, Don, and slips out of the car. She links her arm through Oscar's, which to others says either Mother and Son or Madame et Gigolo circa Paris in the Sixties. It's never been clear.

The gallery is privately-owned, bijoux, pinned between a gentleman tailor's and a ladies' boutique. Not far from here, when it's daylight, Abercrombie & Fitch offer hard-abbed models, Oscar's age but of the opposite build, to punters for snapshots. Oscar used to crave a man like that. Used to stand in the porticos of ambassadors' houses, looking down on the teenaged girls getting Insta-orgasms with the men of their dreams as he sucked on a Mayfair. But hey. *Time fades away*, as Shakey put it.

Before they go inside, Charlotte takes out a pack of Vogues and lights one up. It's white as the moon. She must be nervous to be smoking.

'How are you, darling?' she asks, breaking their link to put her arm around his shoulders. 'Are you alright?' From her tone, there's more to the question than Yes or No.

'Yeah. Why?'

'Nothing, it's… You'd tell me if there was something wrong, wouldn't you?'

There's nothing to say. It's anyone's guess what's wrong with him. But Charlotte's picked up on something, might even know exactly what it is. Whereas she used to say things like *You'll get over him* and *Terry didn't know how lucky he was,* nowadays she limits herself to vague questions. Because whatever it is, this jelly-boned glumness, it has to do with her. Or something far bigger than a boy who left, anyway. And she knows it.

Charlotte tilts her head, blows her smoke away from him. The sky is black, depthless. 'I'm going to quit,' she says, wagging the fingers clasping the cigarette. 'Last time today, I swear it.'

And then, a vibration from her bag against his hip. The default iPhone ringtone, sounding like the soundtrack to a TV jungle show.

Somebody wrote that. Someone else OKed it.

'Sorry, darling!' Charlotte answers. 'Just got here. Coming in now. Literally, just outside. Alright. Bye-bye.'

As she slips her phone back in her clutch bag, a demented person comes running out of the building towards them. Xandra. That tiny, frantic woman, Tinkerbell on speed. Her shoes scuttle down the steps, machine-gun rat-a-tat-tat, her spiky red hair pricking the night. A whole fucking moon on her collarbone, made of sapphire. She gives Charlotte a hug, and it lingers. 'You look an absolute dream, darling!' she says. 'Come in, come in!' Then she turns to Oscar, eyes not quite narrowing enough as she smiles. 'Hello, sweetheart,' and a squeeze of his shoulder. Makes him flinch inside.

Xandra links her arm through Charlotte's and the two chatter up the steps into the venue. The women have been friends since before he was even born, seen the men go in and out of Charlotte's life until Oscar came along to end the parade. Behind Xandra's back, Terry liked to call her Belgravia. He smirked as he did so, as if he wasn't from Chelsea himself.

Inside, Charlotte's mint and jasmine float off to the high Georgian ceilings. Beneath them, a mosaic of bodies and clothes and fragrances. As she makes her way through the room the buzz of conversation grows, friends, acquaintances, publicists, editors, booksellers and agents all reaching out to touch and schmooze. Her hand meets each in turn. It's all his vision can process now, body parts segmented from the whole. That's what's changed. Charlotte has become a cluster of pieces to him now, everything has. None of it fitting together.

Cross-processed photos in frames along the walls. Bellinis and White Russians clinking in cheers in front of them. Low black tables, polished almost to glass, bear little black bowls of cherries on legs as thin as a high-heeled shoe.

People come up to Charlotte, who introduces Oscar as her son. Never even pauses. (When Belgravia does it, she allows a brief silence, cold enough to shrink balls.) But people aren't here for Oscar, they're here for his almost-mother. They ask questions about the writing process and if the movie rights have been bought for this one. Benedict Cumberbatch should be in it! Colin Firth! Is she working on the next in the series? She needs to bring Alicia back, such a diverting bitch! But mostly, everyone tells her she's beautiful, and Charlotte, after a blink, strokes their arms in gratitude.

One of the voices swimming around is a man's. 'You made it,' he says, a smile on only half his face. 'You look stunning.'

Charlotte peers down at her dress, feels the fabric between her fingers. 'It's gorgeous, isn't it?' This is a trait of hers, to pass a compliment along to its rightful owner. To turn a remark on her beauty into a pat on the back for the seamstress. But in her heart of hearts she must know what she is. At her age, she has to. Thanks to glossy magazines and the rise of Helen Mirren, Charlotte's become the face of The Older Woman. The role model for every quinoa-and-kale-eating housewife who can still feel her labia.

The guy's half-smile grows into a full one. He wants to shag her. It's all too *Harold and Maude*.

'Darling, I'm so sorry we're late,' Charlotte carries on. 'I'm afraid my boy was out playing, and forgot the time.' She winks at Oscar, then puts her arm around him. 'Oscar, this is Tim Kielty. Tim, Oscar.'

'Hey, Oscar.' The man not only offers one of his hands to shake, but covers Oscar's with the other. Takes the boy by surprise.

'Nice to meet you.'

'Likewise.' And when he smiles again, there's a small gap in the man's teeth, where one is chipped.

Riding along with Xandra's rat-a-tat heels comes the scent of a manly cologne. Alec, the husband who makes husbands jealous. Glass of wine in one hand, wife in the other, and Charlotte in his sights. 'There's our answer to Chekhov,' he says.

Charlotte smiles back, a cousin of the smile Xandra uses on Oscar. This is their charade, Charlotte the patient nanny to Alec's cheeky schoolboy. 'Darling!' she says, 'I'm so glad you could come.' And she doesn't quite touch him as she pecks the air by his cheek.

The women resume their chit-chat, which Charlotte soon interrupts to introduce Tim. Turns out he's the guy who's taken over foreign rights and translations of her books. Belgravia gushes at him about French, the poetic syntax of it, Rimbaud, the wonderful summer she spent in Provence, while Alec turns from the others to bore into Oscar. 'And how are you doing, young man?' he says. Man's got a stare that won't quit. He looks at every female as though he's already had her, but he looks at Oscar as though it's only a matter of time. He's charged with sex, could run the O2 off it. Salt-and-pepper hair, grey eyes, pec-definition clear through the Jaeger shirt. It's all Oscar can do to keep from sneaking looks at every part of him.

Yet the thought of a night with Alec is the opposite of welcome. There's something dirty about the guy, in a Westminster-scandal kind of way. Bella has an expression for men like Alec— *You might die if you had sex with him.*

The words ring in Oscar's ears.

Outside, the smoke of his Mayfairs blows back into his face. He should change position, but physics was never his strong suit.

A couple walks past across the street. They try to keep their voices down but it's clear they're fighting. The man looks concerned, forced against his will over something. His wife (lover? sister?) is sour-faced, hands flying. They remind him of Lauren and Andy, his previous foster parents, back when he could only count to his age number. The couple looks nothing like them — unless Lauren and Andy lost a bet to a warlock in the past fourteen years — but there's something there that invites comparison.

Lauren had a straight fringe and a penchant for motivational fridge magnets.

Andy had a Kiwi accent and bowling-ball calves.

These aren't so much memories as a flashed-out Kodak slideshow in his mind. That flat in Putney — the newsagent's below — the swimming fish on the 3D toilet lid — Lauren's eyebrows when Oscar clocked Andy in cycling shorts — her alarm when she caught him in the wardrobe, trying on a dress. He was eight, she was apoplectic.

And one October day, a different kind of woman opened her home to him. *My name is Charlotte, and I'm very happy to meet you, Oscar*. She never once asked to be called Mum, and the boy was instantly smitten with her face and shoes. Charlotte was the calm that had eluded him in his first few years. Moved him gently by the shoulders from polyester to lambswool and he became her good little boy. While his school reports were grim, she put no pressure on him to be, or to achieve, anything. As long as he didn't sell meth in the playground, he could never let her down. *Not everyone can be Stephen Hawking*, she'd say. On their seventh anniversary, she taught him how to apply eyeliner, during a time in his youth which it now mortifies him to think was Emo. Another year, she bought him a lads' mag for giggles. How she laughed at the burger-nipples on the fake boobs…

On turning back to the gallery, Oscar's body freezes. Goosepimples.

The guy is standing outside, the foreign rights and translations guy. Tom? John?

He loiters in the light of the street-lamp, smoking. Doesn't look like a cigarette. Too small, thin. Wacky, maybe, though the guy doesn't look the type. It's only when they're a foot apart, Oscar on the way back into the building and the agent politely stepping aside with a friendly *Hey*, the scent of leather and mandarin close to his face, that it dawns on him. The man is smoking a cigarillo. What a kook.

Inside, another thought dawns. The man had been watching him out there. Who knows how long for?

03 SUPER-8

Eight a.m., startled awake by a torrent of bangs. The sound of Polish and hammering out on the street. Waking has always been finger-snap quick for Oscar. It's how a tramp must sleep, on the defensive, as if he might get knifed at any minute. As though his days of being tossed between suburban foster homes was a time of leering 'uncles', rather than the Catholic hemlines and sensible shoes that it was.

Out of the workmen's radio come the yodels of Alanis Morrisette, to which an accented man sings along, only to be cajoled by his colleagues. Oscar should lift himself up and stagger to the window, have a gander at this no-doubt beefcake in a vest who knows all the words to a woman's meltdown. But the sun burns through the window, and his sweat sticks the cotton sheets to the backs of his thighs. The Eye is around his neck, having spent the night with him. Could've been deadly. One false move in his sleep and he'd've been choked to death like an heiress in an Agatha Christie.

In the sitting-room, legs folded on the sofa, Charlotte's looking all Brigitte Bardot. Hair clipped to the back of her head, a few rebel streaks left to hang as she writes. Every morning, she rises to greet the sun. Drinks a tall glass of wheatgrass juice, goes for a jog around the neighbourhood, is back at the flat by eight. Then she stands at the kitchen island to slice up a grape-fruit before getting down to work. The two-seater sofa is all the workspace she needs. It's adjacent to the window looking out at the street, where foreign au pairs stroll by with prams and blazered children. Charlotte surrounds herself with cushions as she scribbles the next bestseller into Moleskine journals, their pages scented by her cream-lacquered hands.

She never looks up when she's working. But on sensing his presence, her smile grows warmer, spreads wider, and wills him to come over and sit down next to her. The tickle of the rug on his bare feet. Charlotte's non-writing left hand on his knee, its gentle squeeze. The skin of her cheeks, softened to the same texture as those fabric covers. The grapefruit on her breath, so distant it's almost sweet. When was the last time he told her he loved her? Does he even feel it anymore?

The apple-green cushions take the weight of his back, and when Charlotte stretches a pinkie to stroke his hand, everything else, as always, fades.

Some girls on the tube shout about which of them got more pissed last night. Sounds like Joanne, absent legend, was the winner. Peed in her own shoe before blacking out on a bus to Kilburn. These are the kinds of chicks that scare him. Young, vital ones. Muffin tops, tramp stamps. Leggings under nothing. Was there really a day when girls were dainty, made of Nottingham lace?

He's on a slippery slope to Meninism. Bella would slap him for these thoughts, this nostalgia for the gentlewomen of yore. Even their undergarments left everything to the imagination.

He's old in the head. A big gay Tory. Just another white, middle-class male who's upset the world has changed. Suffragettes tied themselves to carriage wheels and lit the match on Cinderella's bra. And, even if he isn't the type to troll a female on Twitter, it makes him nervous.

Charlotte reads those doorstop Victorian novels. Stories in which society ladies can't even mention their heartburn for fear of a great-aunt choking on a Peach Melba. Then she goes and writes books about uptight housewives erupting with lust over a showerhead.

No-one on the tube has what Xandra would term *a classic face*. Either DNA was cooler in the nineteenth century, or it all boils down to hairstyles and daguerreotype. Blue eyes blanche in sepia. Humourless men turn sinister. Ghosts, hard as stone.

Terry took a selfie like that once. Gave it a filter to make it antique. It was a picture Oscar pored over, his reaction a blend of fear and love and sadness. As if Terry had happened before, was once the same man in a slightly different body (because how many variations can there be of the same features— eyes and nose and mouth?). And Oscar has happened before, over centuries, millennia, as a waif and a wretch and a whipping boy. Sometimes gay and sometimes not, but always with an air of doomed hope and hopelessness. A tangle of nerves waiting to be untangled.

Five Eastern-European guys laugh and chatter as they sway by the carriage doors, muscles flexed from gripping the handlebars. The world is full of men, and it keeps replenishing. When it kills them in wars or sends disease their way, or pushes them out to other lands, it makes others to compensate. How would it feel to touch someone new? To bury his head in another chest, stroke a different arm, smell another nape? One of these lads, for instance.

It doesn't feel right somehow.

He should put some music on. Dig out his headphones, play some Sarah Vaughn or Janis Joplin. But nothing jumps out. No album, no artist, no song on the playlists. Even Shuffle would feel like a parody. Nothing can summarise the day, give it a theme to work towards. No thing can express this intangible mood.

On Millennium Bridge, a breeze flicks around them. Bella likes to gaze at the water, and dream of the sailors who lived and died at sea. Blue John, she calls it. A boatload of schoolkids passes underneath, so she waves at them. 'Why are they always German?' she says. A sudden gust of wind knocks the cloche hat off her head, but her little white hand darts out in time to pin it back. In the split-second shock, she's gorgeous. Lovely and glowing. Nothing like ten minutes ago, when she read another e-mail off her phone, and turned to announce she'd failed to get the museum job. About an hour before that, she was rejected by a gallery.

The river and the passing footsteps on the bridge fill the silence between them, until she breaks it. 'Remember the whale?' And at his blank expression, 'Oh come on, the whale! The one that lost its way and got stuck in the Thames for days. It was, like, a million years ago but you're not that young.'

'Oh, yeah.'

'Fuck, that was ages ago…' She looks down at the rolling water as though the mammal is still trapped in it, searching in vain for the sea. A smile lights her face. 'Lukas and I saw it together. He was probably — I dunno — eating a sandwich or checking out a jogger. But I saw it.'

A sky full of clouds, and the brickwork of the Tate against it. That old, old structure, from a time of lace and urchins. The contrast almost stops him from speaking. 'Do you ever wish people were more… Victorian?'

Through her shades, Bella is blinking. 'You mean, as opposed to this *Madmen*-meets-Nirvana aesthetic we've got going on?'

'Like, if people were more… you know, genteel.'

Her forehead creases. 'Get your head out of the clouds, Pisces. The only people who were genteel back then were loaded. More than our parents, even. And it was all just an act for other posh gits. Behind closed doors they were spanking their tea-boys and getting syphilis from teen prozzies.'

The Mayfair droops at his lips. 'Everybody?'

'Every last one of them. You know they used to check hookers on the docks for STDs? Never bothered to check the sailors who had a go on them, though, did they?'

Another gust of wind rattles the bridge at their feet. Bella braces herself against the weather. 'What council-funded eco-wanker designed a bridge made of Sprite cans, anyway?' On the trudge across the river, the wind rolls back and forth, kneads the water. The people who walk towards them, families, loners, tourists with bumbags and Canons, struggle against it. It weighs them down, moulds their faces. Oscar's sunglasses form a vignette around the oncoming bodies, mute the sunlight and the colours. Everything turned into a moving filter. Polaroid. Super-8.

Bella's right. A hundred and fifty years ago, the Tate was a factory. Kids would've worked in it, lost limbs and died.

St Paul's diminishes behind them, seeps through layers of atmosphere 'til it looks as 2D as a Turner. A cathedral high as God. As impressive to contemplate and as easy to forget. There's the Shard in the distance, even higher, finally finished. The city's own flick-knife phallus made of glass. At London Bridge with Terry one day, the Shard still under construction, he fantasised aloud — how beautiful it would be if the cranes lifted three immense, single pieces of glass, cut into isosceles, up from the ground and joined them together into this tall, tall pyramid. How majestic. But Terry cut him down. Doesn't work that way, sunshine. Architects would laugh if they heard his fancies. The glass façade is made bit by bit, office window hammered next to office window, bit by bit, up and up, until the Shard reaches a point. Logic always wins out in the end.

'So, Oskovich…' Bella says, 'I kind of need to tell you something.' Behind her shades, her eyes narrow. 'You know what, even just saying that now makes it seem like a much bigger deal than it is, and I don't want you to think I'm being patronising or handling you with gloves or whatever, I only thought I should give you a heads-up.' She breathes in, then out. 'Terry's coming home for Christmas.'

What month is it? August? September?

His stomach's gone cold.

'Just for Christmas, though, I think. Then he's off to Malaysia and Vietnam and back to Tokyo.'

'Oh. Right.' There's no feeling in his knuckles. Or his dick. Not that that's unusual, 'cause without the benefit of another's touch he never remembers it's there.

'I'm sorry, Osky,' Bella says. 'I was so wrong about him. I knew he was a douche, I knew it deep down, but I still let you get with him. If it wasn't for Maya…'

'It would've happened anyway.'

She threads her arm through his, which surprises him. Rests her head on his bony shoulder, a skinny cat in need of warmth. 'Well… Maybe.'

The moment's cut short by *La vie en rose*. It's coming out of Bella, who puts a hand down her bag and takes out a phone. She groans, and turns it towards him. Words flash on the screen, *Source of All My Problems calling*.

She takes a deep breath before she answers. 'Hello, Mother. Yeah, I'm fine. I'm with a man. Nobody, just some guy I met online.' She grins at Oscar, nudges his arm.

It makes him smile. And reminds him of how they did meet. That night, the bar in Hoxton.

Terry on a red leather sofa.

Terry and his G&T.

It makes his eyes sting.

'I didn't get it,' Bella tells her mum. 'Because we disagreed on Matisse. How should I know? They just didn't want me.'

Out of the ether, the sprinkling of steel drums. It's coming from beneath the bridge, on the sandy bank that's revealed when the tide backs away. Bella brightens like a little girl, points to the band in the distance. Her face is looking thin, thinner than ever. Her eyes so huge within it. As her mum chatters away, she turns her phone on its side and holds it out to take a picture of the band. Four Jamaican guys in tie-dye T-shirts sway their bodies to the music they're making, while a small crowd bobs and applauds to the music. *Under the Sea*.

As a kid, Oscar was convinced he had Ariel's hair, that they were hair twins. Red, not ginger. Ginger was the word spat out by other kids. He tried to sing like her too, but was lacking that wave crashing against his back. Not to mention the lung power. When Ursula sends a phantom hand down the mermaid's throat, steals the glowing orb of her voice-box, followed by those two seconds when Ariel grabs her throat — it gave him chills. Poetry. *The poetry is in the pity*. Terry never saw what affected him so deeply.

Bella ends the call. 'Huh,' she says, deleting the snaps she's taken. 'There goes Plan B for a career.'

The music tinkles on as a breath swells inside him. Terry's coming back. Ariel's here.

There's a German word for it, that state of being in awe of what you don't understand, but it's not in his head anymore.

That fell out too, along with the rest.

The window of the cab is open just enough to let a breeze tickle his hairline. They're saying it'll cool down soon, the Met office or whoever. A white Christmas may be on the cards. After this spell of heat it seems unlikely, but there's always the pleasure of hope.

There's the sound of static and incoherent babble. Don the cabbie replies into his walkie-talkie, information that eludes Oscar, being that it's spoken in Northern.

The mystery of his own accent remains. Must've had one in the days before Charlotte. Belgravia would size him up in the early days, when she dropped in for a cup of Earl Grey and a chinwag. Her eyes would linger on him as she beamed her congrats at Charlotte. *You can't even hear it anymore!*

Hear what?

Nothing, darling.

Was it a lisp? A noisy jaw? A whistle through his teeth?

There was something in the woman's tone, the faint gratitude in *You can't even hear it anymore*. As a child, passed around the suburbs, Oscar must've had an accent. Of some kind. Maybe a

Kiwi twang from Lauren and Andy. After those afternoon teas, Xandra safely out of the door, he'd fire the same question, again and again, at Charlotte.

What did she mean? What can't you hear anymore?

Oh, it's nothing, darling. Xandra's only being silly.

If he'd been looking at Charlotte's face, it might've assuaged him. But he'd been looking at her eggshell shoes, and the twitching toe spoke volumes.

He should've traced his real mum. That was the plan, when he was younger. But the teen years drew to a close, and the desire to find her ebbed. A reunion would be grim, Ken Loach. She'd be twelve years older than him and walking the streets of Leytonstone, face caked in make-up, arms covered in track-marks. Fuchsia dye-job. Or she'd be well old and working in an Oxfam in Derby. She'd call him *duckie* and neither of them would raise the question of how the fuck she birthed him.

Once upon a time, his vowels were either blunter or wider. Belgravia kept records, a regular Henry Higgins in Comme des Garçons. His past lies somewhere, swimming in his marrow, dormant in his DNA. If he knew what it was, he might even be able to access it, tune in. It scares him to think it mightn't be so.

Don has learned not to even try chit-chat with him. Not because he expects rudeness or even coolness from Oscar, but because the boy's a verbal dead-end. Instead the man drives with the radio on, switching between talk-channels and pop charts. Against the leather seats of the cab, hypnotised by the passing Georgian blocks, Victorian statues, Katy Perry, right-wing callers incensed by immigrants or the shadows moving across the back of Don's seat, Oscar is lulled into drowsiness.

But it's this drowsiness that's crying out to be captured on a track. This *kleine nachtmusik*. Sounds like dim guitars, over a snare thumping from the other side of a wall. Something's going on somewhere, just not here. If only he and Don could break beyond the centre, beyond Zone 2, if they went up Seven Sisters, past the Middle-Eastern restaurants and bakeries, past

Arnos Grove and got onto the A1, the vastness and promise of the motorway... If only the wanderlust were there.

That's what Terry resented in him. His lack of ambition, his contentment. The fact that he'd never even thought of leaving Charlotte. But how could he understand what it meant to have stability? For even an hour not to be in flux?

Terry's in Tokyo now. The city that got bombed and built again. Bigger, louder, brighter. A mesh of skyscrapers and haute couture, video-game arcades and studio flats. Actual fucking robots. He might be sitting on a bench, eating noodles from a Styrofoam tray, watching the blinking neon signs. His legs crossed on the concrete. (It's silly shit like that.) He'll take the bullet to Kyoto, spend his weekend walking hand-in-hand beneath a canopy of cherry blossoms with an Asian mother's son.

And by Christmas he'll be here. Terry, once again in the same city. Apart from him. It makes his gorge rise.

If not out of London, they ought to at least drive somewhere else within it, a place less grand and moneyed. Bethnal Green. Stratford. But the thought of the East End scares him nowadays. There's a tiny voice in the back of his head, and it — for it is sexless — whispers warnings about the alleys that attract him into them, and the unmarked cabs that suck him in. This boy with elfin features, delicate as a gazelle. Easy prey in those Whitechapel streets. Some Jack could rip him a new one, given the right mood and a lack of options.

That's what he's called, Charlotte's foreign-languages guy. Jack.

No, Tom.

Something like that. Something traditional and English. Old-school, kind of boyish.

Terry's in Tokyo.

The city glides by, past the window, and it hurts his eyes to keep them open for long. Those dots of light in the darkness, coming together in his vision.

Tim.

That's it.

04 SWALLOWED A HORSE

Charlotte thought it might be pleasant to spend a morning with Xandra and Sandrine, Alec's daughter from his first marriage. This was a sometime, maybe daily, pastime, before Sandrine discovered boys, cars and the Grand National. The sight of her robust body among the glass perfume counters at Harvey Nicks is enough to provoke nostalgia. That farm-girl physique, that honey voice. Their childish games in bedrooms, before the age of sexual tension. When she switched from pretend restaurants and Kingfisher ovens to flashing her knickers, the friendship began its fadeout. She tried it on with Oscar once, a sad and hopeless endeavour. Tapped him on the shoulder and took him into the pantry. In the piss-light of the cramped space, to the rumble of the boiler, she lifted her dress without expression and offered no explanation. Oscar was bereft of words. Was Sandrine expecting a critique? Applause? What would Charlotte do? *Mmm,* he nodded. Then, as an afterthought, folded his arms. *Lovely*. Sandrine never showed him her knickers again.

Now she towers above her stepmother, pointing out bottles of fragrance.

'Aunt Char!' she cries when she sees them, and jumps up and down. 'Sorry I couldn't make it the other night, I hope it went swimmingly.'

'You didn't miss a thing,' Charlotte says. And, caressing the girl's face, 'Look at you. Gorgeous as ever.'

Sandrine laughs, almost blushes. She offers Oscar an equally friendly greeting, the same zeal and cheek to kiss, but something feels hollow between them. Their relationship a vintage biscuit tin. Despite the void between them, the youths are encouraged to wander off on their own while the mums shop and gossip. Sandrine takes Oscar by the hand, says, 'Come on. I'm dying to try on a McQueen, but I need an honest opinion. God knows I won't get it from the salesgirls.'

In the womenswear department, Oscar's swallowed by a low armchair while Sandrine fumbles with her limbs and fabrics in a cubicle. When they were teens, she assumed he was comfortable enough with her lady-lumps to invite him to her room, time after time, as she undressed and redressed for a night out. *Come on,* she'd say, grabbing him by the shoulder, *help me get ready*. And he'd recline on her bed all Titian, stomach churning, eyes averted, while she filled dress after bra. His vibe must've been so cool she mistook his silence for sisterhood. Years later, she's still making him pay for his cowardice.

'Well? What do you think?'

The dress is too loud, too flirtatious for her matter-of-fact body. 'Mm. Lovely.'

'Yeah?' She twists into every mirror, a myriad women twisting back. 'I wish I had a nicer bum. I've been doing all this cardio and eating raw, but nothing seems to change down there.'

'At the gym?'

'Hmm?'

'Have you been going to the gym?'

She'd better not ask him to repeat himself again. The effort might kill him.

'Oh. At home, with my trainer.' And at that, her eyes sparkle. When she bends to whisper her confession it's as if they're in her bedroom again, all those years ago. 'Oh my God,' she says, 'and he is fucking *hot*.'

Her arms and legs, all those big bones of hers, surround him.

'Oh yeah?'

'Yeah. I really want to shag him, but I kind of get the feeling he's intimidated by me or something. 'Cause actually he's from

Peckham. He talks all sort of South-London, and maybe like he's exaggerating it actually. So maybe he wants me, too. He calls me Posh Spice.' She grins. 'I do fancy a bit of rough.'

When the children and their mothers reconvene, Belgravia suggests a nice cream tea. Despite the instant hunger provoked by the thought of scones, now's the time to excuse himself. Charlotte regards him with a flicker of disappointment. It's the first time she's ever looked impatient with him but the moment is brief, then gone.

'You're a busy boy,' she says with a light voice. 'I struggle to keep up with your schedule!'

'Oh, Sandrine's exactly the same!' says Xandra. 'Rushing around all over London. She's been to places I've never even heard of. I remember when you couldn't even set foot in the Docklands for fear of being slaughtered. Now they're having parties in former mental asylums, and rock concerts in tunnels.'

She and Charlotte wander off.

And like that, they've released him. Sandrine lingers for a second, eyeballing Oscar. It's a look that says both *I know exactly who you are* and *I don't know you at all.*

In the queue at the newsagent's, Oscar spaced out over rows of Haribo and cough sweets, comes the sound of trouble. There's a man in front of the till, another man behind it. A card reader and the Oyster top-up sign, a charity deposit overflowing with coppers. The man in front of the till is gesticulating, the man behind it refusing to listen.

'I know your kind,' the man behind the till says.

'I haven't fucking stolen anything! Why would—'

'I know your kind.'

'You know my— He knows my kind!'

'You people are always stealing!'

The man in front laughs, shakes his head. 'Oh my days…'

'You blacks always stealing.'

'Un-fucking-believable!'

The accused man turns to Oscar. 'Did you see me steal anything?' he says. 'Did you see me steal anything from this shop?'

But his confrontation makes Oscar go mute. It's the Riots all over again. Smashed-in windows and fires around the city. His heart pounds.

The accused man stares at him as he shakes his head. 'Unbelievable!' he says, throwing up his hands.

Useless tramp.

Debutante.

Snowflake.

With the bed of a princess and the shoes of a pauper.

He couldn't help the man in the shop, couldn't even open his mouth. Should've been awake, should've been *woke*. The man didn't steal anything, of course he didn't. He only had dreadlocks, which made Oscar fear for his little gay life. Poor guy was neither thief nor killer. Brings to mind graffiti he saw in a toilet once, scrawled in biro on the cubicle door—

MY PAKI'S GONNA FUCK YOU BLACK BASTARDS

It scares him, even the memory of it.

He should've been alert in the shop, should've been a standup member of society.

When not with desire, Alec looks at him at times with contempt. As if to say, *Do something with your life. Make yourself useful, you pampered cunt*. If this were 1914, Oscar would be serving his country in battle. Him and a bunch of Tommies, scrambling in ditches beneath a rain of bullets, not doing shots off each other's bodies in Chelsea. And they ask him at those Mayfair launch parties, Charlotte by his side, *What are you up to these days?* which only gets a *Nothing much* back. Then something flies past their eyes, and the question's redirected to his peers. Equally pointless, but at least they've learned to cover it. They could never pay a London rent, not even with a London wage. In a parentless vacuum, they'd all be homeless.

Sandrine would be sleeping in cars, the personal trainer a lingering memory.

Terry's discovering Asia. Maya designs jewellery, flogs it in a Shoreditch boutique with her college friends. Lukas sits for hours on his laptop, making websites and flyers for his uncle's clients.

And Bella. Worked hard for a History degree but can't get a job related to it. A mother trying to push her into the world of Law, where she is, the livelihood that made their lives. Bella's mascaraed eyes narrow at every bit of well-meaning small-talk. *What do you do?* Less an inquiry than an inquisition. Bella's smart. Everyone expects big things from her.

Too many people want to be The Next Big Thing. Get the most followers on Twitter, the highest bonus in the City. As if being ordinary's a crime. If nothing means anything, and death is the end, then surely having been ordinary would be just fine. It'll be OK if Oscar, pointless twat, leaves no mark on the world, once he and it are gone. What difference would it make that someone was a bricklayer, someone was a physicist, and someone wrote a song at fifteen? Britain had an Empire. Napoleon wasn't short. Thatcher and Langston are dead. It is what it is, 'til it isn't anymore.

But now there's pressure to be essential. People and things are expected to justify themselves, European migrants, labourers, medical staff, even public services. Things cost, costs are cut. What Oscar doesn't know could fill the ocean, but at least that's clear to him. Charlotte often seems oblivious of the fact she's an endangered breed, a soon-to-be-casualty of civil war. 'Cause if people hate the rich, then they hate her. And for roaming around, a drain on resources, jobless and witless and dickless, they'll hate Oscar even more. So far he's been a lucky son-of-some-bitch. But things change.

There are times when it sounds heaven to have a job, to be useful in some way. To be a waiter in a small café, somewhere in the alleys of Soho, or Shoreditch. A place that sells tea and sandwiches, all-day breakfast, cakes, baked on the premises. To wrap the sandwiches in cling film, to sticker them, careful to make the all-caps legible with a Sharpie… EGG & MAYO, HAM & CHEESE. TURKEY & CRANBERRY for the month leading up to Christmas. The smell of toast and coffee. Ella Fitzgerald in the speakers. Wake up at seven, have some wheatgrass juice, go for a jog around the park. Chase it with a smoothie or a green tea at home. Get the sort of body that's lean and healthy-toned. No raging pecs, no need for hassle. Just some shapely calves, a little definition. Enough meat on him to look a bit less Lucien Freud.

He might even sing as he takes the bins out — *Both Sides Now, At Seventeen…*

That's all a life needs to be. A place where no-one cares about money, no-one's throwing himself off Le Coq because the share value spiralled away.

All those suits on the tarmac. All the money that pushed them over the edge. Killed by ambition as if it were the Plague.

The neighbourhood looms. Sun on the trees, light through the leaves. A Rorschach on the pavement. Oscar's feet drag him, drunk, Madonna in the *Justify My Love* video. Stumbling from S&M threesomes to androgynous orgies, breathless and woozy with pleasure. Horny bitch.

The flat is close enough now to see that there's a man leaning over the balcony rail, smoke coming out of his mouth. His white shirt is open at the neck, his sleeves rolled up to his elbows, naked arms among the flora. His face unclear, shadowed.

'Hey, Oscar!' the man calls, spotting him below.

Tim. His name is Tim.

There's nothing to do but say hello and go inside. Join him on the balcony. It would be rude to leave a guest unattended. In the cool relative darkness of the building, Oscar's eyes take a while to adjust. The new porter greets him, lifting his head up from the Telegraph, and hurries over to call the lift. Princess. Debutante.

In the flat, the sound of Carolina washing up drifts out of the kitchen, the chatter of Charlotte's Radio 4 blended into it. Sunlight fills the sitting-room, the dining-room, up to the ceiling roses and the chandeliers. Daubs of colour on the walls.

The man is framed by the balcony doors. He's still watching the neighbourhood, the birds, as he smokes. When the doors click open, the agent holds his cigarette — cigarillo — at a distance, and wafts the smoke away.

'Y'alright?' he says. 'Charlotte's in the bath. I'm a bit early. And, er— Carolina, is it? She said she'd warm your food up if you're hungry.'

'Oh, yeah. Thanks.'

'Tim.'

'Yeah.'

The man grins. 'I've been ordered to wait here,' he says, and he points with his eyes and eyebrows towards the kitchen.

Carolina hates this English habit of not allowing smokers to smoke inside. Every time she takes out a Marlboro and shuts the doors behind her, the affront blazes on her face. Tim's misunderstood her, assumed her anger was aimed at him, when it's really aimed at The System.

The man leans on the railings, lights another cigarillo. 'You smoke?' he says, then he lights up one of Oscar's Mayfairs. The ashtray has already been brought out from behind the barrel planter, and Tim slides it closer to Oscar. His arms are peach in the sunlight, freckled, the hairs fine. He's wearing a Swatch, loose on his wrist. Clockwork visible behind the plastic. It's cute. Alec wears a Mont Blanc.

For a while there's only the smoke between them. Tim is squinting, whether from the sunlight or the fact that he's stuck on a third-floor balcony in Kensington with the only plant ever called Oscar. His skin is almost Charlotte in texture. Younger, but still worn. And yet this thirty-something, bent at the waist next to him, was once a boy. Must've been at uni at some point. Must've had a tricycle and a school tie, and a bag stained with sodden lunch. Must've sat exams. Had a first kiss.

'What the fuck...' Tim says, squinting no more. His lip pulls up in a half-smile, baring a few of his teeth. The chipped one, the aperture in his mouth. Below, a woman rolls by on a scooter, Whole Foods bags swinging from her arms as she shouts after her wayward, equally scootered children. Tim laughs, shotgun loud. 'She has to be over forty!' he says. 'Is that a sample of West-London parenting skills?'

And it strikes Oscar for the first time that Tim isn't from here. The way his vowels swell every now and then, that's not from any end of the capital. But now's not the time to quiz the man about his origins, or draw attention to the accent that marks him out.

'There was this lady once...'

Tim looks a little surprised, even relieved, to hear speech from the boy.

It encourages Oscar to continue. 'An old lady. She was dressed in a fine hat, like she was on her way to a wedding, but she was carrying a baseball bat.'

What the story lacked in content, it made up for with molasses delivery. But somehow it's tickled Tim, and he laughs again. A chuckle this time. Less an expression of surprise or amusement than appreciation, as if the anecdote went exactly where he wanted it to. There's a beauty spot above his lip— on the side that doesn't rise when he smiles. Like a pin, keeping his mirth locked down on a single part of his face. His nose swoops, a sudden halt at the tip.

He's looking at him.

The look's too loaded to be accidental. Not like the split-second shame on the tube when your eyes flick up to meet a stranger's. Oscar is being screened by the man, assessed. Tim's eyes travel downwards, brighten at Oscar's neck. 'Hang on,' he says. 'That's an Evil Eye, in't it?'

'Yeah... I got it in Camden.'

Tim nods, and takes a drag of the cigarillo. 'I love them,' he says. But he doesn't go on to explain what they are. He must assume Oscar already knows. 'Hey,' he says instead, 'd'you want to hear a story?'

'Always.'

Tim smiles, and changes position to face him head-on. 'OK… So, I was travelling around Greece one summer, must've been about your age. And I met this guy at a taverna in Kos, where I stayed for a few days, a guy called Thanos. I often saw him at that place. We sort of… kept catching each other's eye.'

Madonna stumbling through corridors.

'We got to talking, and eventually Thanos became a friend. He was a laugh. And really, passionately political. Totally right-wing but so charming you couldn't even hate him. Anyway, one day he invited me to his mum's house for Sunday lunch. So I said, "Sure." Easy as that. Sunday rolled around, and Thanos took me to his mum's. And, Jesus, she was this tiny, minuscule being with a bit of a hump, and she hugged and kissed me on both cheeks as though she'd known me all my life. Then, swear on my life, she leaned in and stared into my eyes'—he leans in and stares into Oscar's eyes—'and she put her hand on my face,'—his hand hovers at Oscar's face—'and she said, "They've put the Eye on you."'

No heartbeat.

'And I said, "Who?" She said, "I don't know, but somebody wishes you harm." So she begged me to let her remove this curse, and I looked at Thanos, you know, like *What should I do?* But he only gave me this look that said *Just do it and get it over with.* So I agreed. The place was… How can I describe it? Crammed with icons and crucifixes— and the old lady sat me down in this wooden chair in her kitchen and put a white cloth over my head. What do you call it, that… cheese-cloth? Then she got a Bible out from somewhere and started to read from it. In Greek, obviously, so I have no idea what she was reading. And when she finished her ritual, she told me I would go to sleep, that I would feel really tired but it was OK. "You will sleep exactly half hour." That's what she said. "Exactly half hour." And you know what? I was tired. Utterly, utterly tired. Like I'd been drugged. I'd only met the poor woman ten minutes earlier, she had potatoes roasting in the oven and I couldn't keep my bloody eyes open! Thanos, poor lad, he had to help me into bed. And you know what? I slept for exactly half an hour, and when I woke up… I felt fantastic.'

Oscar's eyes are billboards. He's a kid back in the classroom, and the teacher's singing about an old lady who swallowed a fly.

She swallowed the spider to catch the fly
I don't know why she swallowed the fly
Perhaps she'll die.

Oscar's mouth is as open as the old lady's, cats and dogs falling in. The menagerie of a search party she's sent in after a goddamn fly. He was always disturbed by that song, worried for the old lady's jaw hinge. Afraid of her, yet freakishly in love with her at the same time— here was an old lady who could swallow a motherfucking horse. And this Greek one had felt the presence of Evil, put her hand on Tim's head and sucked it out.

'Obviously I don't believe in it,' Tim says, dragging on his cigarillo. 'I actually checked my pockets when I woke up in case it was all a scam. I s'pose that's what London does to you. But I have to admit, it's stayed with me. I mean, exactly thirty minutes, too… She must've hypnotised me or something. An old Greek mesmerist, you know?'

Oscar's mouth is twitching, but no sound comes out of it. Tim thinks him a cynic, that Oscar is judging him. He should say something.

'I mean, I don't think anything supernatural happened,' Tim carries on, cigarillo back in his mouth. He blows the smoke out into the clear sky. 'But I like the idea of it. That the story ever came to be. And I only came in about halfway through.' He leans down, diminishing the space between them, stubs out his cigarillo. A strip of sunlight turns his hair to cinnamon. Then he's standing up straight, tucking his shirt into his trousers. 'Anyway,' he says. 'That's enough rubbish. Let's go inside.'

He and Tim are barely in the sitting-room when the man starts talking politics, something to do with the House of Lords and trade agreements, Britain's possible exit from Europe. He clearly doesn't know the boy — there can be nothing down this road but trouble.

'Uh ...'

'Yeah, I think that's the general view.'

Before either of them can say anything more, there's the sound of Charlotte coming out of the bathroom. The dull click of that door shutting, the bright one of her bedroom door opening. Moments later, her footsteps along the corridor until, finally, she enters the room. Light and fresh as foam. Charlotte, rising from the bathtub like Venus from the sea. An image Oscar once thought heavenly, until Bella told him the goddess was born after her dad's balls were cut off and his jizz rocketed into the Med.

Charlotte apologises for detaining Tim, but he insists he was early. The Moleskine journals are stacked neatly on the white coffee-table, the corner of one crushed, pressed in like the skin of an elbow. Shabby chic. That's what Charlotte's skin is. She smiles, brings Oscar closer to her and kisses his head. 'I trust you've been a good host, Oscar-darling.'

Politics can wait.

'It was fun,' Tim says. 'We even caught a scooter chase.'

A hint of confusion in the woman's eyes, but she works it. 'Ah! How fortunate!'

Tim can't look at her straight. His gaze is on the carpet, close to Oscar's shoes. He rolls down his shirtsleeves, inch by inch until his flesh is hidden. It's the thought of her damp hair against her supple skin, or the image of her rising and sinking in the foam. Younger men tend to be flummoxed by older women. As though they're a different species, a mysterious upgrade from the girls in skirts in bars, to tiptoe around and faintly dread.

Outside, Tim smoked a cigarillo, spoke of Evil Eyes and grinned with half his mouth. Inside he's got his hands behind his back, having stood up to greet a lady, and his smile is a thin line. A handsome tin soldier.

PJ Harvey's *Dress* plays around Oscar's head, dances on his lips. The Holy Mother's spirit has entered the room. She watches from the *Rid of Me* poster, icon above the fireplace where Charlotte had once hung a mirror. That fuck-you stare. The wet hair, whipping around her head like a monochrome rainbow. Music used to be everything. There was a time when a song could open him up and work its way in. These days it's too much effort to take the headphones out of his pocket. Maybe he should invest in a chunky over-ear pair, the hipster staple of the Overground line. In this present state of mind, even putting on *Dress,* his ultimate Going Out tune, is too much work. Going Out feels like sarcasm.

His clothes are sprawled on the bed, tiny personas in waiting. But his head's cloudy, can't think straight. The scene in the sitting-room plays on a loop, Charlotte and Tim, him and Charlotte. Only minutes ago, yet it already feels like ancient history.

It wasn't just Tim— Charlotte was altered too. She pulled Oscar into her bosom, made a human shield of him, then all but kicked him out of the room. *We have business to discuss. Go play with your Barbies.*

No. Why think that about Charlotte? She'd rather eat McDonald's than throw Oscar out of anywhere.

She was freshly scrubbed, smelling of soap.

And yet, there was a look in her eyes, familiar from everyone else but her. It said, *Please leave.*

Tim was reduced to a boy.

Now there's a boy in Oscar's mirror, white shirt unbuttoned to the tits. The Eye at his chest, his legs in black skinnies, his feet in leather ankle boots. Dress happened without his even being aware of it. Life on autopilot.

The ensemble says nothing about him anymore. It isn't what it feels like.

He should get back into music, consume it like he used to. Songs, lyrics, vocals, artwork. All around his bedroom wait kicks up the arse. Sophie Calle hardbacks, Weegee, Floria Sigismondi, Graciela Iturbide, Vivian Maier. A photo by Diane Arbus, of a woman eating a sword. Viktor and Rolf promos. A Basquiat print. Gig tickets forming a second frame around the mirror. Past highs, once stimulants, now as distant as the first time he went down a slide. He used to sing into his mirror, used to dream up lyrics and type them into Notes on his phone. Record his voice and play it back.

He should dye his hair again. Back to that poison-apple red. Or blonde, like Veronica Lake. Or dark, like Morticia Addams. But maybe that would only look *Twilight*. The last thing he needs is the stigma of Emo.

Tim probably laughs at Emos. Laughs with half his mouth.

No-one even looks at Oscar on the tube.

Outside Angel station, a girl — living Photoshop of Boy George and a Tim Burton movie — hands him a gig flyer. Seven bands in one night, each of them made up of people's mates and boyfriends and colleagues. In the back end of an Islington pub, where the beer on the floor sucks the shoes off your feet, and the sound drills through the speakers above your head. Could be fun. But probably not.

Terry took him to such a dive in Kilburn once. Everything was corduroy and lank hair. A disco ball above the stage, a set of random curtains, Fifties kitsch, a booze-stained floor and the smell of coats drying. A folksy duo from Birmingham took the mic, sang about love as an oven glove and bellybutton fluff while strumming a xylophone. The girl's eyes scraped the room at every quirky lyric. Two-and-a-half songs were more than Oscar could bear, by which point he was overcome with the urge to leave. *Where are you going?* Terry said. *I've got something in my eye, it's like ...* To his credit, Terry tried to look concerned. But Oscar went to the gents' on his own, with the niggling feeling that he'd managed to piss his boyfriend off. Half an hour later, he was still in the toilets, which annoyed Terry more than the made-up eye trouble. In a room whose measurements amounted to six feet, A4 posters of Nineties nostalgia nights on the walls, a toilet missing its seat, graffiti conversations on the door, *MY PAKI'S GONNA FUCK YOU BLACK BASTARDS,* in the stench of urine, between puddles on the ground and around the sink, that old familiar sadness descended on him. Who knows when it first appeared? Maybe it was always there, dormant in his head, a chemical ash cloud waiting to gather. But this time it took longer to pass. The thought of Terry's face, the folksy duo. The girl's eyes scraping the room. Terry's look of delight, then his concern at Oscar. The faces around them. The beer in the air. The chatter. *Something in my eye.* Terry turning back to the music. It all seeped into his body, waterlogged its every part. Made him dumb. By that point, he and Terry were already coming to an end. In hindsight it's clear as glass.

It can't be. This, still. Terry is gone, been months now. Several weeks, many moons ago, like the Spice Girls and Florence Nightingale and Charlemagne. It's over. He can't keep reliving a bad romance.

Terry standing at the bus stop, feet crossed like a ballet dancer.

Terry in his beanie, reading the Metro on the District line.

Why, when Oscar was on the brink of a different attitude at last, a plan to carve a career in the hospitality industry, writing TUNA or HALLOUMI on sandwiches, must a boy resurface in his life to wipe it all away?

A job is what he needs. A job will take care of him, and Angel will provide. The N1 centre is in front of him, and people are pushing from all directions. He's incapable of movement. Hobbled. How is he going to get a job? Why would anyone give him one? Bella has a degree and is still unemployed. Sits stewing at home or rages on the streets at anyone with a clipboard getting paid by the hour to ask her to empathise.

No. He'll get a job.

But he should've dyed his hair first, scrubbed up.

There are shop fronts and restaurants everywhere, so much glass in which to check himself out. And it's tragically in the window of a Tesco Express, on the other side of which a wench shovels Krispy Kreme doughnuts into a box, that the image of Oscar Present confronts him. A person gaunt and haggard, hair the opposite of L'Oreal. All cheekbones and eye-paint. The death mask of a camp Egyptian pharaoh.

Maybe gaunt and haggard is good. Maybe it says 'hardworking' rather than 'smack addict'.

Before he knows it, the target café is in front of him, waits for him to step inside. His throat is dry. His mouth creates saliva, forces it down his gullet — a fleshy machine — but nothing. His heart beats faster. They'll hate him. He'll fail. This place couldn't be cuter, a toy café with steps leading up to its narrow door, red-and-white chequered tablecloths, miniature people on their tiny laptops with their little Descartes paperbacks in some infant girl's dollhouse, on her cloth-and-papier-mâché street of antique stalls and fashion boutiques.

His hand is gripping the Eye around his neck. Tim's story comes back to him, that woman in Greece with a cure for Evil. It makes him breathe a bit easier.

Inside, the café is relaxed. Only dunes of loners scattered around the small room. The walls are magnolia, adorned with crocheted cats and chickens. Gig posters. Flyers of film nights and art shows. A girl sits with a pile of textbooks, her head in one hand while the other makes notes in a pad. A guy in a dark coat and corduroy trousers sips his coffee by the window, eyes wide and staring at nothing, like he's just been landed a blow. A ring of spilt coffee around his cup.

'Can I help?' says a girl from behind the counter. Buddy Holly specs and a pinched face. Her colleague turns too, cut from the same cloth, to look him up and down.

'Um… Do you have jobs? Like, vacancies?'

'Manager's out now,' Buddy Holly girl says. 'You got a CV on you?'

Fuck. A CV. 'Oh… N-no.'

The girl laughs. 'OK…'

The other one gives her a look.

'Have you ever worked in a caff before?'

'No, not really…'

There's the smell of charcoal from a burnt tea-cake. A sticker of a badger on someone's laptop.

'Well, I don't know,' the girl says with a sigh. 'I mean, you could bring in a CV and try your luck, but I don't think, like, I think the manager would probably want someone with experience?'

'OK. Sure, yeah. How do you get that? Experience.'

'Uh… I don't know… Bring in a CV, give it a bash.'

Both girls wait for him to say something more, or *please leave*.

'OK… Can I have a flat white then, please? To drink in?'

Buddy Holly doesn't answer, just turns around and starts brewing the coffee. The other girl tops up the cakes and cookies on display. Before long, a cup and saucer of different pastel hues are set down on the counter before him. 'That'll be two-fifty then,' says Buddy Holly.

'Yeah. Sorry, thanks.'

'Oh, yeah, there's a five-pound card minimum.'

There's no change in his pockets. The girls are staring at him, as though there's something on his face, dead and sliding. The vibe of the place has changed, the energy, whatever it is Maya would call it. He doesn't know why, but it's clear that he should just go home.

The girl awaiting payment shoots daggers at his hands, the crumpled notes in his fist. Her eyes flit between Oscar's face and his cash. And they're narrowed. Why? Because of the way his notes are kept, scrunched up like a bad idea? So what, bitch? It's only cotton. A fifty with the queen's face on it. Stick a wad of notes in a washing machine, watch them ball up into a soggy clump. It's still a thousand pounds, wet or dry, crumpled or ironed. Moody bint. The sudden anger overwhelms him, shocks him.

'Haven't you got anything smaller?' she says.

'No. Sorry.'

'Well, I haven't got enough change in the till for a fifty.'

'Um...'

'There's a cashpoint at the Tesco near the green. You could draw out something smaller.'

'OK... uh...'

He could add something else to the bill, get up to five pounds and pay by card, stop the bleeding.

Then again, there's no reason why he should. 'The Tesco, yeah?'

First Girl points him in the right direction, impatient. She doesn't know he won't be back.

People excuse themselves around him, negotiate their way past. Others are closing shops or market stalls, or standing in groups outside the pub. Beer in their hands, smoking outside. Ash from their cigarettes flicked into the air. The street rubs against his feet, the soles of his shoe worn down to a mere suggestion. He really ought to buy new shoes. Charlotte's bound to notice, if she hasn't already.

What a twat, thinking he could waltz into a place and get a job. Without skills, without prospects. Came to stand before those working girls, shirt unbuttoned like a boyband tosser, and demand a job. Posh-boy wanker. No wonder they hated him.

Maybe prostitution is the key. Build a customer base, get a steady income. Work a nine-to-five, pm to am. Service ugly old men with unspeakable needs.

Down by the green, strangers' faces are turning up to look at him. Someone is humming, and the sound is close. Really close.

It's that song, that familiar song. Something about Ferris wheels. Joni Mitchell.

It's coming from him. The shame of it shuts him up.

At Tesco, the cashpoint speaks of many thousand pounds in his bank account. More than it was yesterday. Must be the first of the month, Pay Day from Charlotte.

Tim must think him a douche. A waste of a private education. The shame is so thick it weights his head.

The sun has drifted downwards, cooling everything left in its wake.

05 YOU KNOW HOW YOU KNOW

'You know how, when you meet somebody — doesn't have to be a lover, it could even be just somebody you become best mates with — and you happen to have the same interests? You're like, "Oh, I like Beyoncé," or whoever it is you like, and they go, "Oh, me too," and it's as though you were meant to meet?'

'Coincidence. Queen Bey has many subjects.'

'Bella!' Maya whines. 'I haven't finished.'

'Sorry. Continue.'

'OK, so you meet somebody and you're attracted to them, like, without reason? Doesn't have to be sexual. Why is it that you go for the person, out of all the people in the room, who is the most similar to you?'

'Ego?'

Maya rolls her eyes. 'OK, smart-arse, not "why" but "how come"?'

'I've noticed the band name on their T-shirt and I have their CD. Turns out we're both into angsty pop-rock.'

'There's a whole branch of psychology,' Maya carries on, 'that's dedicated to studying this phenomenon. The idea that people are somehow, like, at a deeper level than we realise, that we're all connected? Like a network of consciousness.'

'Maya, that's very lovely, very *Lion King* and whatnot, but you need an intervention. Anything with "The Science of" in the title, you can guarantee it was written by some woman in LA with feathered hair who sees angels in her massage oils. *The Secret, The Real Truth, The Power of Love,* whatever, all that 'sending vibes out to the universe' while you drink coconut water with Noel Edmonds is a waste of time. Stay away. Scientology's only one step away from that.'

'Bollocks! That's totally different to what I'm talking about. I've seen proof of this myself.'

Bella cocks an eyebrow. 'Proof.'

'Yeah, proof. Back in school.'

'Alright…'

Maya leans forward in her seat, leather moaning, and she drops her voice to a murmur. She slides her eyes between Oscar and Bella as she talks. 'When I was doing my Psychology A-Level, we had this teacher who was a bit of a kook. She used to leave class in the middle of a sentence sometimes, or start singing that *Good Morning, Good Morning* song from *Singin' in the Rain*? So anyway, this woman, Miss Henley, tells us about a new… I don't know, activity I guess? Called Constellating.' And before Bella can say anything, she adds, 'And no, it's not astrology.'

'Damn.'

'Basically, one person in the room is assigned the role of Constellator. They bring an issue to the table, say maybe their parents got divorced, but they don't tell anybody what that issue is. Then they have to use their gut instinct to pick people in the room to represent a person —or thing— from that issue.'

'A thing?'

'Like… an emotion. Say, uncertainty. Or fear. Anyway, when they do that, the Constellator positions everybody where he or she feels in their gut they ought to be. And every time they did so, Miss Henley would ask the people in the Constellation (that's what it's called) how they're feeling, OK? And everybody had to answer. Truthfully. Like, if they felt disgusted, or scared, or in love, or horny, whatever, they had to say it. It's what we *represented* that mattered. And you know what? At first it all started a bit, like, nothing really happened? But when we'd done it a few times and people loosened up, it. Got. Freaky. People were playing out the issue to a T. Without knowing anything about it beforehand. Sometimes the Constellator never revealed what the issue was. They just said everything was one-hundred-percent accurate.'

'Maybe it didn't add up and they were too polite to say.'

Maya sighs. 'Even the cynics were won over. B, we exposed other people's emotions. People who were, like, two or three degrees of separation from us sometimes.'

Bella folds her arms, hugs herself. 'Maybe you picked up on the constellator's emotions as she was moving you.'

'Well, OK, then doesn't that prove our connection to each other?'

'I mean, in a different… You pick up on feelings. We're sensitive beings. Besides, Maya, it was school. You all knew each other. Remember when we found out Freddie's dad was a drag queen, after he was spotted doing cabaret at an all-night revue? We and our mothers knew all about it in seconds.'

'OK, sure, but I presented issues for the Constellation sometimes. Things nobody in that room could've known. I wasn't even friends with most of these kids. We sat in opposite ends of the common room.'

Bella frowns, picks at her long-sleeved T-shirt. 'I don't know… I don't, for example, feel an affinity to that man sitting on his own at the window. But I can tell he's the sort of guy who likes to be alone. Or at least, that he doesn't let it stop him living. He might be a writer, he might have no friends, he might have broken up with his girlfriend… We fill in the blanks.'

Maya nods, sipping her tea, liquorice and peppermint. Something in her smile says she's been holding the big guns, and it's time to get them out. 'OK, genius,' she says, 'explain this one. One time, I was the Constellator. During the Constellation, this girl in the group suddenly looked down at the floor. Just straight down, unprompted. And she was staring at the carpet for, like, a minute. I noticed but I didn't think anything of it. Then, Miss Henley looked at me and said, "Maya, did somebody die?"' She pauses. 'My grandma did. The Constellation was about her. This girl I never even spoke to, she sensed that. She was looking at the ground like she was at my nan's funeral, looking down at the grave. And she had no idea.'

Oscar and Bella are on the bus, going nowhere. One of Bella's Austerity Hobbies — jump on the first bus that comes along and see how far they get before they start spotting too many tracksuits. Two girls in school uniform sit together, a short distance from them. Twelve years old at most. One's hair is braided, and she plays a soulless R&B track on her phone while the other, in a headscarf, nods to the beat.

Bella's right. If he had no idea who she was, and had come up to the top deck to find her sitting by the window with a line cutting her forehead, he'd assume she was angry. Angry about something beyond her control. And he'd be right. She broods next to him, boiling the space around them.

'Do you think it was … What Maya was saying …'

Bella turns her head to him. The sunset in the foggy window tints her ears peach.

'Do you think there might be something in it?'

'Oskovich …' she sighs, 'I love Maya, I really do, for whatever insane reason. But … woman's got a screw loose.' Then, adjusting her top at the stomach, she turns in her seat to face him. 'When I first met her, I thought, "Oh, she's such a doll, cute as a button, we could be friends." And it helped that she was a bit ethnic, you know? 'Cause up to then my life had been so white.'

A laugh escapes him. The mirth is brief, cut short by the fear that the schoolgirls have heard, and think him racist.

Bella smiles. 'But I was different then,' she says, 'before you knew me. I was a bit more accepting. And don't look freaked out, I wasn't *that* accepting. But with Maya at least, because she was so harmless and gorgeous and made of honey, I gave her the benefit of the doubt. When she was a kid, she was a Christian. Like, stoning-Hypatia levels of Christian, probably because of her mum. But then she decided she didn't believe the Bible, who knows why, probably because of her mum, but I could tell she still had it in her. God. The need for God, anyway. It's why she downloads horoscope apps on her phone and does her daily Tarot readings on Facebook and says the things she says. My point is, in school, when she and her classmates were doing those constellations or whatever they're called, Maya was the sort of person who looked for God in the gaps. Still is.' And, looking down at the Eye, she adds, 'She's just as fucked as the rest of us.'

The heavens have opened. Pearls of rainwater slither down the windows, join to form liquid tunnels through the haze. The red traffic lights that stop the bus fracture into mad shapes. Condensation. All those years at school, scraping by and out, and still he couldn't say how condensation happens. Bella would know, but now is not the time to ask.

It's strange to think that the girls have a history, a world that excludes him. Bella knew Maya as a shy, churchgoing waif, not a fashionista who knows every vintage shop in town. Maya knew Bella as a lard-arse, as Bella puts it. Maybe even met her mum. Bella's invited Oscar all over the city, but not once to her family home. He hasn't a clue what her bedroom is like. Probably a creamy double adorned with newspaper clippings. Photos of Sartre and de Beauvoir, with The Other Woman. A fireplace, a hat-stand from the nineteen-tens and several cloche hats from the twenties. A total absence of the fairy lights that normally fringe a girl's bedroom. She, Maya and Lukas might've spent time in it together as teens, Radio 1 playing in the background, as they discussed people at school. They sometimes refer to those people now, reminisce and fall into hysterics about things said and done in the past. Things that often involved Terry. Meanwhile, Oscar was at a different school, speaking to no-one. Coming up with excuses not to play rugby.

The guy in front of them on the bus, hair thick as Nutella, is scrolling through Grindr on his phone. Pics of half-naked men flash between the bus seats, their proximity given in yards. When the bus halts at Brixton, heaving everybody and his grimy seat, the schoolgirls get up to leave. One of them chats about accidentally accepting an invite to another girl's birthday party, a girl she doesn't even like. *I got confused, man*. The quality of her voice changes as she moves away, switches ambience as she exits the bus. The parting of *Text me, yeah?* muffled, bass-heavy.

Passenger after passenger drips on. The bleep of Oyster cards. Footsteps on the stairs, followed by the backs of heads, then bodies, then faces as they turn to look for seats.

The bus lurches forwards and drives on again. At the stairs, a grey shaking head appears. An old broad, her entire body rocked by its own nervous system.

'*Aidez-moi …*' she says. Her voice is creaky as wood.

Bella throws her arm out, keeps Oscar from getting up. As if they'd emergency-braked and she was the driver. She doesn't look at him, doesn't move her arm from his torso, but continues to stare at the shaking old lady. On the opposite end of the bus, a girl with shopping bags topples over onto her friend. She laughs her arse off, *Sorry!* And her friend laughs back.

The shaking old lady makes her way to the back of the bus, struggles to keep her balance. Her eyes are wet. '*Aidez-moi …*' She's inches away from Oscar now, but doesn't even know he's there. She repeats the words, even when she's taken her seat in the back row.

Bella moves her arm away from him. 'I can always tell the crazies,' she says, breathing a sigh of relief.

Oscar's heart is pounding.

The guy checking Grindr lifts his head from his phone. At the same time, another guy, further up, turns around to meet him.

Cheapside shrinks the sky. Cityboys rush past him in their own Grand National, pinstriped, coiffed and scarved. Some of them sit on stools at Prêt A Manger, side-by-side staring out through the glass, spooning minestrone out of paper cups and into their mouths. The reflection of a bus travels into and over their heads.

A horn bleats from amongst the traffic. It bleats again. *Aaaaaaaaaaaaaa*. Half-sheep and half-machine. It's so otherworldly that people look around for the first time in months. But their eyes meet buses and cabs, other frowning faces, and no answer. *Aaaaaaaaaaa*. One of the Cityboys mimics it, but he amps it up, so close he's nothing but a face bleating into Oscar's as he approaches with his pinstriped friends. Whiskey on his breath. Everyone looks at everyone else, amused and baffled. They talk with their eyes, the way folk do in clubs, when music drowns the conversation and they want to ask the guy across the floor where he stands on cubicles. A beggar's dog barks at the noise, causing more commotion. A sign by its owner's feet about working for food.

BANK. The tube sign in red, white and blue. A black-coated mass of bodies pours down the stairs to the station, and Oscar's too far in the middle to fight his way out. May as well sink underground with them. But there are so many bodies, and he has no idea where they're taking him. The steps going down seem to come right up, and every one is aiming for his face. A guy on his right, flecks of grey in his stubble. A woman on his left wears a baseball cap, eyes concealed. Nose broken, reigned in by elastoplasts that stretch across her face. There's the swishing tail of a skirt in front of him. His shoe on the steps.

A flash of skirt, a shoe, a step.

Skirt, shoe, step.

Skirt, shoe, step, skirt, shoe.

One false move on his part and this bitch'll go flying.

Underground, the terror of stairs in the past, the bodies crisscross in front of him. Central line, Northern line, Circle & District, DLR… He ends up in a white-tiled corridor, the sound of heels clicking in an arc, a spiral, all around. The smell of piss, perfume and bleach. Damp black coats. A thread hangs from a woman's skirt, tossed to and fro in the scissor-cut chaos of her legs.

Alec works in the City. Might even be one of these hundred people around him. Sharp suit, pounding his way through the white-tunnel crowds, knocking the dentures clean off a rival's face.

Charlotte's agent, meanwhile, would be sitting in a cosy office in Pimlico, or somewhere off the King's Road. Exposed brick-work and skylights. Or not. Might be one of these horses too.

At last, there's an escalator. Pot-bellied CEOs surround him, wheezing above the mechanical whirr. The guy in front checks his Blackberry. No signal at this depth. The fluores-cents sweep across the moving stairs. They brighten the grey ridges, and Oscar's feet, then vanish. They come again, then vanish. Something struggles in Oscar's throat. It dries him out, the need to swallow.

Terry hated the DLR. Said it felt like a toy kicked across the floor by a child. But Oscar only saw a sort of magic in its driver-less glide amongst the tower blocks. Its high-treble sound and the lights of the buildings, a journey as a funfair ride. Like trav-elling inside a giant box TV.

Analogue, man. That's how old he is. There are kids who've only known digital. *I remember when you didn't get WiFi on the tube*— that's what his generation will be saying, months from now.

The train stops, West India Quay. As good a place as any.

There's no-one else on the boardwalk. Instead of the moon, the water is lit by fluorescents from the office blocks. And it's pretty. Prettier than in real moonlight, probably. Something about the contrast, the natural and the manmade. Unless that's something Londoners tell themselves to curb the thought of black mucus clogging up their airways. Bella mused about it once, while they were crossing Blackfriars Bridge beneath the blackest sky of the whitest stars. Right there in the Big Smoke, stars as clear as lit-up tube signs.

The bright spots from the tall glass office blocks dance on the water, this dark body that splits the city, seen by him and the tourists and the ancient tribes that chose to settle here. This mass that divides him on the boardwalk and whatever drone is working overtime in that there office. Sending an e-mail, uploading a video, using the lights that reflect on the river and blur in his eyes.

This must be what Tokyo looks like.

Terry hated the Docklands. Canary Wharf, West India Quay. The old-school names that evoke boats and sailors and opium dens to Oscar were only soulless commercial monsters to Terry. See-through castles and Armani suits. Fancied himself a separate entity, a Prole. He'd start rants about the downtrodden working class, tried his best to befriend anyone in it. But where they live, he never dared to go. Only ventured where they used to call home, years after the men's clubs and factories became wine bars and gelaterias.

Terry's out there somewhere, awake or asleep in a different time zone. Also staring out at a body of water. A foreign river cutting through a foreign landscape. Is he thinking of him, too? It's Maya and her constellations again, those invisible phone wires between them, between them and everybody else. Human bodies as phones, sending messages through a nervous system. And if memories play on a loop in Terry's head too, does he see Oscar at the bar, on the night they met, in the neon web of lights? Does he see a pair of startled eyes? The first, mannered conversation. The swapping of phone numbers. The princely kiss when they parted ways at the station.

Terry playing games on his phone on the tube, sometimes Scrabble. The two of them passing the phone back and forth, struggling to turn letters into words.

The awkward standup they saw on a canal boat in Little Venice. The hilarious drag queen after that.

Don't you want to find your mother?

The reluctant kisses.

Aren't you even curious?

The suitcase on the bed.

Boxers drying on the radiator.

I'll miss you, I'm sorry.

The Oyster card slapping the barrier.

Terry vanishing from sight.

Ne me quitte pas, ne me quitte pas…

If only he missed Oscar, even a little bit. Nobody wants to be easy to leave. Not for Tokyo. What's so fucking great about Tokyo? They were in London. Walked along the Wall as the sun was coming up, tipsy from the free booze at a friend's degree show. Kissed in Highgate, after Oscar revealed his fear of death. They were on buses and trains, once on the DLR. That's where their conversations and their feelings, the imprints of them both, together, remain. Every spot in this city holds a portal to that former life. He only has to stroll down Old Street to hear Terry go on about *The Walking Dead*. Only has to use the Central line to feel his ex play games on his phone next to him.

Maybe that's what drove Terry away. Everywhere held remnants of Oscar and him (at least it does for one of them). Terry had to leave this city, start afresh in a different one. London had nowhere left to go.

Ne me quitte pas.

Those words, Jacques Brel's voice. This is the way songs have come to exist for him — in his head, cut up, rearranged, samples that play and repeat at random. It doesn't mean anything. A song is a song, and a bit of its memory got spat out. Brain signals and whatnot, cables tangled in a box TV.

Or maybe the songs that play in his head are messages. SOS, from the old Oscar to the current one.

The water moves, dark and constant. *Died of a broken heart* — that's what they used to call suicide. Cityboys falling from Le Coq in Armani suits. Died of a broken heart.

The Eye is cold in his hand.

Ne me quitte pas.

The night's gone black and turned the tube windows into mirrors. When the DLR takes a bend, in the backward slide of the lights on the glass towers, a reflected face behind him looks familiar. Tim. Or his döppelganger.

Oscar should turn and say hello, if that really is the man. It's not like it's impossible, even in a city chock-full of souls. See a stranger in a leopard-print coat on your way to Leicester Square, spot the same gal on a train back from Hampstead six hours later. Somehow, the odds work in favour of You and Them, and never mind the other eight million city-dwellers.

Before his mind's made up to say hello, the face in the glass is gone. The train's stopped and the man, Tim or not, walks past along the platform towards the exit. Something about that gait, the back of the neck, the ears. It was Tim. If only those few seconds hadn't separated them.

Moments like this, Maya would call Fate. Things happen for a reason, according to a plan, managed by karma. Tim was brought to Charlotte. Oscar happened to buy an Eye, which attracted Tim's attention. Tim happened to go to Greece, years ago, and have a story about the Eye to tell. And even before that, the seed — Oscar happened to be fostered by Charlotte, who happened to have a weakness for doe-eyed cast-offs. Oscar's real mother happened to have birthed him, to have had sex with whomever and a lone sperm managed to impregnate her and create this being. Does she know, this faceless mother, what he's become? A creature whose pace is slow, whose eye is readily caught, whose attention gives out halfway over a zebra crossing. Who could spend a full minute waiting for a hand dryer to come on before realising it's a paper towel dispenser. Is she the same? A dim twat? Will they both get mowed down by a cyclist and know, feel each other's pain like twins?

Bella insists on brushing aside what she can't explain. But the truth of the matter is they were brought together. Bella and Terry and Maya and him, Charlotte and him. And now Tim. They were all linked in the ether, joined up in the stars, before Oscar was even born. Before Tim was born. A boy who grew up to be this man, given to cigarillos and Fahrenheit. That's what his scent is, the mandarin and leather. Fahrenheit.

He looks good, too. Wouldn't burst any thermometers, but you wouldn't say no, either.

The tube stops, and the doors slide open. In the reflected faces, a boy, about the same age as Oscar, ambles in search of a seat. Huge grin on his face. He chooses the seat next to Oscar, of all the seats, and falls on it, having had no time to get cosy before the train took off. He's a mess, every one of his limbs working to get his headphones in his ears.

There's the tinny sound of salsa music in the air, but that's coming from the middle-aged Asian guy behind them.

'Breeeeaaaak a leg,' slurs Drunk Boy, still fiddling with his earphones. There isn't even a hint of music playing in them. 'Yeah. Yeah, breeaak a legh.'

He raises his hand. He's going to slap the shit out of him.

Instead, the boy makes a show of hitting his own knee, but misses and hits Oscar's instead. 'Breeaak a leg, you fucker, your… you in mud… shoot.'

His hand rests on Oscar's knee. All is still between them for a while, dark all around outside. The salsa music rages on in the older man's headphones, gets downright saucy. Drunk Boy moves his hand at last, puts it in his pocket. His elbow slams into Oscar's chest. 'Snot my car… Who's… ?' Keeps slamming.

Charlotte's going to be called in the morning. Identified as the next of kin, in the wallet of the corpse found pummelled to death in fucking Shadwell. The boy's hand flicks up, clipping Oscar's chin. It's finally happened. Violence from a stranger. The Revolution starts.

The boy turns. 'Oh, pardon me!' He has an accent, Irish or Scottish. 'Pardon me.'

Now the boy's staring at him. And smiling. He has a Muppet face, neither cute nor ugly. Its thick, near-triangular eyebrows are raised, and there's a mole beneath his red-rimmed eyes.

'Are you OK?'

'Pardon me.' He tries to put his headphones in again, but keeps looking back at Oscar and smiling. Bashful. Must be a bottom. 'What's that?' he says. 'Yeah, I'm dandy. Dandy.'

'You sure?'

'Dandy.' The boy smiles, looks away, then looks back again.

Oscar should help him. The boy might be in trouble. 'Where are *you* going?'

'Ahaha … No, no … Where are you going?'

'Home.'

'Ah. That's nice. How is … Where is your home?'

'Kensington.'

'Ah, Kent.'

'No, Kensington. Do you think this train is for Kent?'

'Kensington.'

'We're on the DLR.'

'I know,' the boy smiles, 'I got on at Westferry. I'm not a … spaz.'

The word makes Oscar's hair stand on end. Who knows what this boy will say next? So many minorities around them.

And suddenly, the stranger's coyness dissolves. Drunk Boy's body is possessed by a Moulin Rouge dancer. He pinches Oscar's nose, all coquettish. The scent of rum between them, so close it's almost in Oscar's mouth.

'Sure you're OK?'

'I'm dandy, me. Can I come — join — Can I join you in Kensington?'

He's homeless.

'We can work something out. You and mean. You and me, can work something out in Kensington …'

He's a rent-boy. A pissed and homeless rent-boy.

His hand goes to Oscar's knee again. 'Kiss me,' he says, leaning in. 'Kiss me.'

The hand crawls up his thigh.

'… I have a wife.'

'Aha …'

'Her name is Charlotte.'

'Ah well.'

The hand is on Oscar's buckle.

'We have a child. He's autistic.'

'So?' The boy is smiling.

'…'

'So what, man? Come on. Come on.'

He fiddles with Oscar's shirt button. Oscar's skin tingles, despite himself.

'N—no. No, we can't, no.'

'Yeah yeah yeaaah…'

All of a sudden, the boy stops moving.

His breath stops too, his smile gone. He's glaring at the Eye around Oscar's neck, as though confronted by an old enemy. Frowning, he turns away, fumbles with his headphones again.

The boy's been wounded, offended somehow. Tower Gateway's coming up. He can't be left alone in this state. In Tokyo, people have breakdowns on public transport all the time, but you aren't allowed to talk to them. It only spotlights their shame.

'Hey… Are you OK?'

'Me? I'm dandy.' The boy turns back and, as though nothing happened, his smile returns, full-beam. It's a welcome sight, even if his teeth are small and crooked. It lifts his eyebrows and brightens his ashen face. He leans forward. 'Let's work something out in Kensington.' He plants a soft kiss on Oscar's neck. It makes Oscar shiver, like a sprinkling of cold water on his naked skin. The boy starts to lick around the Eye's cord. Rum on his breath. 'Go on…'

Across from them sits a Pinstriped Boss of Somewhere who clears his throat, frowning at the whole gay spectacle. Oscar's steeped in embarrassment. He should explain. Just a look to explain that his role in this is purely Samaritan.

The DLR comes to a halt. Tower Gateway. Everybody wakes up, packs away the books and iPads, and heads for the doors.

Someone has a blue plastic bag of oranges. Pinstriped Boss is already out of the door.

With a demigod's strength, the boy grabs Oscar's arm and yanks them both up. But, energy spent, he can't sustain himself. He leans into Oscar, refuses to let him go.

'We have to get off now.'

The boy cackles.

'We have to go.'

'Your wife and kids? You wanker.' But he's smiling, and pinches Oscar's nose again. 'Autistic, yeaaah? He can draw us an air—plane. OK, Kensington. OK, get off.'

'Are you going to be OK?'

'Dandy. You wanker.'

'Sure?'

'Dandy. Get off.'

From the escalator, Drunk Boy looks even smaller as he stumbles out of the train carriage. One of his headphones has made it into his ear. The grin is still on his face, and those triangular eyebrows are still raised, as though Oscar never even left.

06 THE KIDS ARE ANGRY

He's woken by the hum of voices through the walls and his bed. A smell of baked pastry. One of the voices is Charlotte's, her laugh warm and melodic. The other is Tim's.

There've been mornings where Oscar's mind has felt outside his head, his head off his body. As though he'd died in the night and was now a restless spirit in purgatory. Today his body is light, but more in the way of a balloon than of a ghost.

In the kitchen, Charlotte and Tim sit at the square oak table, giggling over the babble of Radio Four. Tim looks up at Oscar in the doorway. His eyes are bright, startled. They flit to Oscar's torso. Charlotte, whose back has been turned, swivels on her chair to face him.

'Morning, darling! Did we wake you?'

Tim's got up from his seat to greet Oscar, but now it's awkward. They know each other too well for handshakes but not well enough for hugs. The expectation of touch fizzes between them.

Charlotte guides Oscar into her empty seat as she puts the kettle on. The shadows of her fingers on the toaster. 'I've somewhat overcooked the croissants, I'm afraid! But they're not too bad, are they?'

'Not at all,' Tim replies. 'They're just right.' Then a wink in Oscar's direction.

This is something every man over thirty seems to be doing these days. The till-guy at Londis winked at him the other night, having tossed the Mayfairs on the counter. He looked Middle-Eastern, but that can't be a reason. If a pack of smokes could provoke a wink, there's no telling what a pack of Durex might do.

Charlotte's making breakfast. No Carolina. Must be Sunday.

She urges him to eat what's left on her plate while she lays some more croissants on a tray and slides it into the oven. The pastry flakes under his teeth, oozes butter and marmalade. It makes a mess of his face, right in front of Tim. Today the man is better-looking than before, spikes of tawny hair and a caramel eye in the sunlight. Meanwhile, across from him sits a boy with bits of filo, Lurpak and citrus peel stuck to his face. It's no wonder Tim looks him up and down so. 'So you like Nico?' he asks.

That explains the looking. Oscar's T-shirt. All of a sudden it feels too tight. His hand is playing with the Eye. 'Yeah. It's a cool photo.'

The man smiles with half his mouth. Takes him for a shallow queen.

'I mean, it's not— like, I'm not that familiar with her music... But this photo I liked for its own sake?'

Tim is patient, and nods.

'Oscar made that T-shirt himself,' says Charlotte. 'Isn't that clever? It's an iron-on — transfer — thing. He used to do it a lot, didn't you, darling?'

'Cool,' says Tim.

The way Tim pronounces things makes him smile, even a word as short as *cool*. The thoughts in his head, along with the beat of his heart, slow down. Something —an energy— compels him to move closer to the man. While Tim talks, his eyes come back every now and then to hover at Oscar's mouth. Maya was talking about body language once, how staring at a person's lips is a sign of desire.

But maybe Tim is just perplexed. Oscar has a woman's mouth, after all. The sort of lips a Romantic might've slapped on a nymph.

Besides, Tim seems to stare an awful lot. Makes Oscar feel like he's been caught out in a lie. Maybe the man has a three-letter disorder, and staring blankly is a side-effect of the drugs.

'Join me outside?' he says. He's pulled out a lighter and a pack of smokes.

For a good twenty minutes he shoots the breeze with Oscar outside on the balcony. Charlotte stays in, defiant, won't give in to the nicotine cravings. Doing her yoga breathing or mindful colouring, or however she controls herself. The days are cooling but the sun's still golden. It tints the man's skin, his hair, his clothes. His fingers, loose around the cigarillo, show a lack of grooming. Rough cuticles. Worn, red knuckles. Hardened by fatigue, as though too many phone calls and e-mails at work have drained them. Those fingers, typing. Writing. Feeling.

The stubble on his cheeks and the tips of his hairs glow red. Orange. A fellow ginger at heart.

Has he ever slept with a man? Is that something you can tell from watching a jaw, or a pair of lips closing around a cigarillo? Maybe he did, once. He must've gone to uni, experimented. That's what people say happens. Get too drunk with a house-mate, shit goes down. A guy at school spent half the day yelling *Fag!* at Oscar, and half the summer ball trying to lick his neck. Those supposed straights outside the bar in Hoxton one time, suits rumpled, sipping Desperados. One parting the other's shirt to lick his nipple. A third guy taking photos on his phone. Bromance. All in jest. A defensive label is all it takes to keep a name clean.

Charlotte's Michael Bublé CD wafts outside from the kitchen, and Tim interrupts himself to grimace every time a new track starts. He does it to himself, not for Oscar's benefit at all. Makes it all the more amusing.

They say it might snow in December. It goes around and around in his head, individual words that don't fit together. *Snow. December*. But it'll happen. And Tim will be here, eating croissants or pains au chocolat with them for breakfast, sipping mulled wine by the lit-up Christmas tree in a cosy jumper.

For now he's talking politics, the country's gradual slide to the far right. A blackshirt takeover sneaking in inside a wooden horse. Scotland will break free of her tired old mother, sooner or later, and the delicate balance of the Irelands will tip and cause a mess too big to clear up. 'Imagine...' Tim says, and exhales. The billowing smoke from his mouth. 'All those generations who lived and died in the United Kingdom, a peaceful Europe, and we might be the ones to see it all fall apart. Is it wrong that I'm a bit unsettled?' But he doesn't wait for an answer. 'Well, I s'pose it's not my business. Who am I to tell people what to fight for?'

And he looks at Oscar.

Tim's face changes when he talks politics. His pupils shrink and his irises burn amber. His jaw goes tight. So close to Oscar's face he could touch it.

The man's fervour makes him nod along, charmed. No matter what Tim is saying, his energy, the fight, the belief, is enough to make a person love him.

They're eating scones in a Bloomsbury café, because Bella wants to act as British as possible in preparation for the future witch-hunts. Don't want to rub a new Oswald up the wrong way and end up on a boat to the Scillies. She's checking Facebook on her phone, and reads out a listicle about things both cherished and reviled from the nineties. 'Why should only neo-Nazis get to wear rose-tinted specs?' she says. Then, after a moment's odd silence, 'D'you think I should dye my hair?' She looks up at him, straight in the eye. If only for a second.

'What colour?'

'I don't know... Black? Red, like you used to? I basically want to look like I'm buying up Knightsbridge.'

'So, like... auburn?'

'Yeah...' Then her mind wanders off. She's fantasising about autumnal locks. 'Meanwhile, aren't *you* looking a million dollars!'

This confuses him.

'You look all sort of... rejuvenated. Anything I should know about?' She winks large.

The blood rushes to his cheeks. It almost makes him open his mouth to confess. But he can't. He mustn't. 'No, nothing. Just ... this is pleasant.'

Bella knows. The look in her eyes says she's gathered information. Evidence. 'Well, guess what happened to me the other day,' she says. And after a pause: 'I might have met someone.'

It stuns him.

'Well, sort of,' she says, holding up a hand. 'OK, I'm going to sound like the biggest specky nerd, but I met this guy at the library. Caught his eye somewhere around *The Invention of the Jewish People* and he asked me out. Isn't that simply wild? He's this thirty-eight-year-old Norwegian with a paunch, who could tell you everything you ever wanted to know about Mesopotamia. He's, like, the man of my dreams.'

'He is?'

'Don't look repulsed, Oskovich, They can't all be you.' She puckers her lips, then looks away. 'Besides, who knows when—?' She stops, but her hand had been indicating herself.

The subject has come up before, her and him. After Terry broke up with him, she asked outright if he would ever bend her way. He said he couldn't, and was met with a shrug. *Worth a shot,* she said. You can't fight nature, no love lost.

A silence falls between them, and it occurs to him to say something, boost her self-esteem. But it wouldn't work. When a person is low, nothing you say can medivac them out of it. It's up to them to choose if and when they move.

'We're going out on Friday,' she says. 'An evening of poetry at the Royal Festival Hall. Guess I'll have to buy a new frock and iron my hair.'

She sips her tea and picks at her scone, most of the clotted cream left in the ramekin. While his mind is filled with treacherous thoughts, about thirty-eight-year-olds with paunches, Bella's need to be contrary, she's sitting across from him with a smile on her face.

Why begrudge her that?

The nation's torn in two, change for the better or change for the worse. And both sides think they're right. All those failed revolutions of history, learned in school or on the streets — Guy Fawkes, the miners' strikes, the War on Terror protests, the student revolt of twenty-ten. Oscar had been warned to stay away from Central London after Charles and Camilla were attacked by the crowds. He was on the tube when folks with picket signs and masks started chanting up the escalators, voices echoing around the tiles, *You say Tories, WE SAY SCUM!* Those same people, on the news, on YouTube uploads, kettled by cops on horseback in Westminster. Bottles flying, hoodies and graffiti. A pregnant woman gripping a railing as she cried. Someone wrote ARCHIE IS GAY on Parliament Square. The riots of twenty-eleven were a bigger, scarier beast, a war on society itself. People spoke of children and teens as if they were aliens, terrorists, a newborn Blitz.

Now there's the threat of another world war. Angry Scots who want to be free, rid themselves of the House of Commons. Europe, Britain against the world. Russia, America, North Korea, ISIS, whoever else wants to join the mix. It could happen. Could be around the corner. Chaos happens in a single stroke. The News is not a thing that can be brushed aside anymore, ignored like a flyer. It's handed out at stations, folded out on transport, blasted on phones and zoomed in on tablets, spilling into social feeds, left and right, left and right. Only Charlotte is a haven now, a place where all that matters is the two of them.

Somehow, it became October. Jehovah's Witnesses have set up spots around town to spread the Holy word, in pamphlets with titles such as *Is Satan Real?* and *The Evils of Halloween*. Hands full of tracts, arms outspread, a friendly smile even when the passers-by scowl, they stand, hour after hour. Another failed revolt.

Bella is one of the scowlers. Tim might be, too. The man pops into Oscar's head every time a Witness appears in front of him.

And nowadays, the thought of Tim comes hand-in-hand with a fierce longing. His face, the ginger notes in his hair, the top button of his shirt undone. When he isn't at the flat, every room feels as if it's waiting for him.

Over the past few weeks, some of the tabloids and celeb-rags have hinted at a new romance for Charlotte. For the first time in years, murmurs have bloomed into full-blown gossip. On stands next to headlines of ministers and suicide bombers, there are paparazzi snaps of Charlotte with different men. One her publicist, one her accountant, and one a teenaged *X-Factor* hopeful who's been tweeting his undying love of her. One of the snaps is of her and Tim. And he's been circled, identified and named.

One afternoon, an all-female TV panel show airs. Charlotte's the guest, and she chats about her latest novel, her obsession with cookery shows, female celebs' reluctance to be called feminists. To her credit, she's been wearing the label proudly, before, after and during its status as a dirty word. One of the regular women asks her if the rumours are true, if she's really got a toy boy. The audience whoops in advance.

'That would be telling,' Charlotte responds, beautifully, and everyone cheers.

But 'toy boy' provoked a brief flicker in her eyes. And if her feet had been visible, the twitching of her toe in her shoe would've said it all.

The absence of Tim, in the meantime, says plenty.

On Oscar and Charlotte's fourteenth anniversary, she takes him for an afternoon tea in Marylebone. She gushes at the wallpaper, the china, the finger sandwiches and miniature cakes as they sip their Earl Greys. She's been so excited to have this day with him that she repeatedly touches his arm. At times, the look she gives him is almost painful. As if he might evaporate at any moment, or die.

The waitress brings cakes and sandwiches on a tiered stand. 'Oh, I think you can have these ones,' Charlotte says. 'It's easier for you to keep the weight off than it is for me.' She puts both of the mandarin cheesecakes, and both the pistachio sponges, on his plate. His favourites. There's a tension in her posture, as if she's prepping herself for something. This is where she'll finally tell him. Here, by the American tourists who find this all so quaintly English, she's going to say it. *I'm with Tim.*

Or something even more insane. *I've adopted Tim. You are both my sons.*

Instead, she bends for the gift she's been carrying around. Wrapped in thick paper, all art nouveau waifs and swirls. Plump ribbons, piled on top of each other like cream. She passes it to him across the table, watches as the ribbons come apart in his hands, and the paper falls away. Her face is pinched with concern.

A laptop. A brand new Macbook.

'It's got Logic Pro on it,' she says with meaning, but the meaning eludes him. 'The man at the Apple shop said that's what you'd need.'

The gift is a mystery, has no bearing on his life. But she would be so broken if he didn't say something, if he didn't at least pretend to be dazzled.

'This means so much ...'

And before he can finish, she claps, makes noises full of glee. Like the time he was a sheep in the Nativity, having failed to land the role of Mary. Charlotte leans over the tea, propelled by relief, and her arms wrap around him and squeeze 'til his eyes water.

Her body against his. This is how it feels for Tim.

In the Reading Room at Claridge's, Tim sits next to Charlotte. Burgundy shirt, Swatch on his wrist. Behind him is the marble fireplace and rows of other tables and wine glasses.

Xandra's in Marc Jacobs, a Cartier iceberg at her cleavage, and Alec's in Valentino. The charcoal suit was a good choice, what with the white shirt and champagne tie. His salt-and-pepper hair. It's hard not to watch the neck that stems from the collar, the Adam's apple bouncing on the tie-knot, the bumps of his nipples through his shirt. He sips his Chianti, careful not to splash his stubble. He licks his lips a lot, sometimes flicks a grin at Oscar, mid-argument with Tim.

'They only want to go to uni so that they can get away from their parents and get a thousand pounds a term from their loan to spend on booze.'

'That's an unfair stereotype.'

'All stereotypes are based on truth. Most young people spend all their money on getting pissed.'

Tim laughs his low chuckle. 'Don't you give Sandrine pocket money? Doesn't she go out and get pissed?'

Two grand a month. And every day.

'Yes. But she's my daughter and it's my money. It's not "borrowed" from taxpayers' money, and we all know that for most graduates, that's a debt that will never be repaid. These kids all want something for nothing. That's what they've been taught. Go to uni, become a lawyer. Doesn't matter if they've got the IQ of a horseradish — that only gets them more things for free! "I'm dyslexic, give me a laptop." That's the mentality.'

'Darling …' Belgravia says, eyebrows fumbling.

'By that same token, "I'm a royal, get me into St Andrews." Never mind the two Ds at A-level. A dyslexic might actually be a first-class scientist.'

'The royals are a different story, I won't indulge that argument. I think we both agree they're a waste of space.'

'I think you're confusing William with Harry, Tim,' Belgravia interjects.

'My point is,' says Alec, 'regular, ordinary, mediocre kids are told they can have whatever they want, simply because they want it. Never mind if they don't deserve it, or lack the aptitude or talent for it. Look at me. I built my business on my own. Granted, my parents helped—'

'Yes. You were privileged. Most kids aren't.'

'But I never got anything for free. Not until after I made my money, ironically.'

'You were given opportunities for free. Some kids don't ever get an opportunity.'

'Oh, listen to yourself! Opportunities! You sound like every lefty with a flipchart I've ever met. Do you want to know what some of these street kids do with opportunities? I'll tell you. They squander them. I'll give you an example, shall I? My company once invested a huge amount of money into a scheme to build decent community centres for people in Tower Hamlets. Hackney, or somewhere like that. Dalston. We built them a gorgeous building, it had…'— and he counts off on his fingers —'…state-of-the-art music equipment. A gym. Performance spaces, you name it. Stunning place. We give it to the kids, and what do they do with it? They trash it. Instantly. Millions of pounds down the drain, because they'd rather take the music equipment for themselves, as though they always had it coming. And I know, all said and done, I call a spade a spade, it's a British problem. I'm not saying it's just the immigrants—'

'Oh, well, as long as it's not the Poles…'

Charlotte raises her hand like a white flag. 'Please, let's talk of something nicer. It's Oscar's special day. Let's leave the talk of immigrants and the EU out of it.'

But Pandora's Box has been yanked wide open. It's *The Cook, The Thief, His Wife and Her Lover,* right here at the dinner-table, over remnants of pork and salmon. Helen Mirren. A roasted man. *Start with the cock.*

'It's pretty awful, though,' Belgravia says, nodding. Alec throws his head back and rolls his eyes, huffing, but she carries on. 'You've got to admit. I mean, here we are, a nation in economic crisis, so many unemployed, and they're just giving out jobs and benefits to any old person coming in from the EU.

Many of them criminals. I'm sorry, I mean, I'm not a racist in the slightest, you know me, but I think we should prioritise British workers. Shouldn't we? I mean, is that unreasonable?'

'Doesn't your son work for BP in Nigeria?' Tim says, as though he's been ready with it. 'That's a much better job than a Croatian barista's. Or Carolina,' he adds, thumb pointing to Charlotte. 'Should your son be asked to leave Nigeria and come back to his own country for work? Would he take over from that Croatian in Starbucks, or Carolina's mop?'

'It's not...' Belgravia smiles at Tim, patiently, but her cheeks are flushed and her eyes flit about.

Charlotte looks down at the table, but her back is straight and her head is raised.

'A person has to be right for the job he gets,' Alec says. 'It goes back to what I was saying earlier. You can't push mediocrity up the ladder just because it ticks a box. Someone's simply being from Croatia shouldn't automatically guarantee him a job over an English kid, because the company wants to tick diversity boxes on forms. Most of them can't even speak English properly. What good is that, if you can't even understand what the employee — the representative of a company — is saying?'

'When was the last time you heard an English kid speak English properly?'

Bella's mum complains of that all the time. About Bella.

When Charlotte opens her mouth to contribute, she slowly raises her eyes from the table. 'I think Alec and Xandra do have a point, Tim. Our country is in deep financial trouble now, and there are so many disillusioned and unemployed people who feel as though their degrees and training and efforts have all been in vain... It's not illogical to believe they're the ones who should be prioritised — yes, over other EU nationals — when it comes to getting a job in their own land.'

Tim shakes his head. He can't stop himself. 'No. No, that's The Daily Mail talking. And if you believed everything you read in the Mail, you wouldn't ever step outside. Statistics have shown that migrants—'

'Let's change the subject,' Charlotte says. She's gone cool as a glass of champagne. 'Poor Oscar's had his ears chewed off with all this.'

'Oh, no, it's fine. Really.' That voice, higher than anybody seems to have expected, makes them all turn to stare at him. Everyone forgot there was a five-year-old girl in the room, holding up her pastel drawing of a unicorn. Partly because of Tim's exasperation with the others, and partly because everybody's waiting to be rewarded with something, Christ-almighty-something, from the boy, words come out of him before they've been screened. 'When did the first immigrants come to England, anyway?'

It was as straightforward a question as *What was the Beatles' first single?* But everyone at the table has taken it for sarcasm.

Tim grins with half his mouth, and watches his own hand play with a knife on the tablecloth.

Charlotte sips her Pouilly-Fuissé. She looks slighted. Her cheeks are red, full of blood.

'You've been hanging around this lefty too long,' Alec says, eyes sliding from Oscar to Tim and back. Then he laughs, genuinely tickled, as he sips his wine.

Back at the flat, Charlotte gets Carolina to assist her in setting out finger-food and cheeseboards neatly on the table, tops up the drinks. While it's normally a calming, almost spiritual, experience to watch Charlotte smoothen a tablecloth, now it's making Oscar feel wretched. A mixture of regret and resentment sloshes around in his stomach. He should've helped. Not just stood there, having everything handed to him. The privilege.

His stupid words at the restaurant. Charlotte avoiding his gaze after that, sullen and almost speechless.

Tim looking pleased with him.

Charlotte slices cubes of brie, camembert and stilton with the cheese knife, arranges the pieces on the board so they look prettily haphazard. And even though there are plenty of reasons to feel for her, to want to hug her and remind her she's loved, there's only one persistent thought in his mind. The woman is a cougar. A cradle-snatcher.

'Have you been using your hand cream?' she says.

'No...'

'You should, darling. It's starting to get cold.'

But she doesn't meet his eye. And it's silly how it affects him, because she isn't his mother, nor will she ever be.

Why didn't she become a mother, anyway? What happened in her life that made her foster a ginger cast-off in her forties, raise him to a Motown soundtrack? Who for? If not in a Brangelina effort to house the world's destitute, then why? It's easy to picture the girl she used to be. The surface of her, the landscape of gentle undulations, softened by time but well maintained. Those soft lilac eyelids. The lines on her cheeks that sank into permanent dimples. The sharp jawline, a touch mellowed over the years. Her age should have lessened her effect, but instead it's united her features, made them stronger.

She must have driven the boys wild. Climbed out of her window in a pencil skirt to meet some dude on a motorbike. Or sat in a bathtub with her blue-jeans on, 'til they shrank skin-tight to her legs.

Charlotte at a party in the Seventies. Farrah Fawcett hair, patchouli on her neck.

Charlotte in the Sixties. Miniskirt. Sunglasses, bigger than her head.

Charlotte in the Fifties. Defying her parents, playing music by black artists on the record player.

Before the picture takes her right back to Covent Garden flower-stalls and the Boer War, it strikes him that Tim is of a generation between him and Charlotte. He was around with the Hacienda, Thatcher, the Soviet Union. But his world is more like Oscar's — iPhones and YouTube, GIFs and tablets. Charlotte came before VHS. Maybe even the NHS. What could they see in each other besides his youth, her beauty? They must have nothing to talk about.

Maybe Tim comes over to spend time with Oscar. It would explain those long, absentminded looks, the frequent glances at his lips.

The two of them walking along South Bank, weaving through the German Christmas market. A flat in Bloomsbury, or Hoxton Square. Oscar's coffee-table photo books taking up the room. The tiny hairs on Tim's jaw and on his cheek, coming closer, towards him with the shirt collar loose at the neck. More of those soft brown hairs revealed as he unbuttons…

Charlotte has been watching Oscar, all this time or for a mere few seconds. She's searching him for a clue. Those eyes, blue as her Wedgwood tea-set.

Jolene.

A cloud of white fig from the candles. Pinot glowing red in a glass.

Jolene.

When she remembers, she spreads a smile across her face.

Jolene.

The men have cooled down since the restaurant. They talk in the sitting-room, Alec asking Tim about his investments with interest, an almost fatherly concern. It's an odd war, this friction between men, akin to magnetic fields. Charlotte seats herself, legs together, on a futon by Xandra. For a long moment, the chatter washes over Oscar, some of it sinking in, most of it rolling off.

'…The sofas are this ghastly ochre colour, this patterned, awful… ugh! Really hideous, and they really don't go with the rest of the room. I'm afraid she's lost her mind…'

'…They went under last year…'

'I'm so happy for her, really, it's so good to see her doing what she wants.'

'Buy some art.'

'…You know him, stubborn as a mule!'

And then Tim's voice cuts through it all. 'Hey, Oscar,' he says, 'fancy a smoke?'

The others moan. Talk of health risks and the general shitness of cancer-sticks. As though they're about to impale baby pandas with them. But nothing could've got Oscar off his arse sooner. Charlotte's bought herself an e-cigarette, and takes it out for a vape, or whatever the term is, to show them she can smoke inside without getting cold or ostracised.

She watches as the French doors shut behind them.

Oscar should've done it first — got up to smoke outside. It would've been a good test. Game-playing is for tweens, but it would've spoken volumes if he had led the way for once, and Tim had got up to follow. It would've clarified if Tim wants to be with him.

Or maybe this says the same thing. Tim felt the need for a smoke, to be outside, away from people he clearly hates, and he chose Oscar's company. He could easily have come alone. Tim bent over the railing, smoking, turning to light Oscar's fag, bitching about Alec. He sought the ally in a room full of rivals. And it's a pleasant feeling, when one of your own calls you back to the pack.

'He talks to me as if I'm a kid,' Tim says. 'Like those alt-right zombies in comments sections. He may as well call me a snowflake. An idealist.' He scowls as he briefly shudders in the cool air.

'Is that bad, though? Like, being an idealist?'

Tim struggles to suppress a yawn. 'I s'pose not. I mean, I am one.' Then he turns to stare him down. 'Do you know how Alec got his job? The former boss was a friend of Daddy's, that's how. And he lectures me about kids who can't even afford the bus ride to a job interview, who wouldn't even eat if it weren't for food banks.' He sighs. 'Sorry. I needed to vent.'

'It's OK.'

Tim smiles, looking a little embarrassed. Their arms are resting on the rail, inches from each other.

'He doesn't intimidate me. He wants to, though. Cityboy wankers with their cock-measuring contests. But you know what the trick is, Oscar?'— it's bliss what his accent does to that last syllable. What his Fahrenheit, on top of soap, and sweat, does to the night air. (And he said the word *cock.*) — 'You recognise that everybody's just a body. Brain, organs, blood, meat. No-one's anything more than you are. It's just that they've bought into their own propaganda. Remember that next time you're dealing with a wanker.' There's a trace of bravado in his tone, a teenage boy with a knife or a condom. He cracks a smile, takes another drag of his cigarillo. 'Sorry,' he says, 'was that really patronising?'

That chipped tooth. The half-smile.

The lights from inside illuminate part of his face, make a patch of stubble shine red. The movement of his head, his hands, seem unreal. Android. But he's real. He taps his fingers and blinks, and there's an eyelash on his cheek that he brushes away before Oscar has the chance, and that action alone, that half-second sweep, was enough to fill the boy with words that can't come out. It's only tradition that's drawing Tim to Charlotte. Old-school thinking, nineteen-fifties mentality, boys and girls and pink and blue. The story could be different, if Tim could only open his mind. Oscar might be the one to make him happy. Tim the one to make Oscar happy. They're only bodies, and bodies, unlike the mind, don't lie. Not even to themselves.

'Do you… do you really think we're just bodies? Or…'

A long silence as the man looks out into the night.

He takes another drag. 'Do you mean, do I believe we have souls?'

'Um… yeah? Is that too schoolboyish?'

'Ha! I don't believe in souls, no. I don't believe in the Soul, or God, or Heaven, or Hell, Purgatory, ghosts or bleeding statues.'

A statue of the Virgin Mary, bleeding. Blood trickling over stone, people falling on their knees. It chills to the marrow.

But Tim misconstrues Oscar's silence. 'Sorry, I didn't mean to be offensive. I don't always know when to shut up. Are you religious?'

'No. Well, I don't know… I haven't really thought about it much.'

Tim nods. 'It's funny. Everyone around here seems to be — West London, I mean. It's like time stopped, because nobody ever got poor enough to doubt, you know?'

'Pardon?'

He stares at Oscar. First the eyes, then the lips. Then he looks away. 'In my experience, richer people are more likely to be devout. I s'pose it's tradition or something, a long line of people whose beliefs have never been challenged, you know? By circumstance, or…. Or maybe it's a guilty-conscience thing. It justifies the Bentley if a Divine Creator meant for you to have it. But on the opposite end of the spectrum, there's people who are so destitute that faith is all they have to get them through.' He takes another drag. 'Sorry, that sounded a bit like I'm going to overthrow the Romanovs. But either way, it's reactions, in't it. The need for God is the brain's reaction to fear. Or that's how I see it, anyway. The fear of there being no real *meaning* to life, that everything's random. Suffering, death, luck, the planet, whatever. Some people don't like to think of the world that way, but I tell you what, I prefer to. I actually find it more comforting. God, the Bible, all that… It has the opposite effect on me. God is a kind of… learned helplessness.'

Sounds like something Bella might say, with a few more *fucks* thrown in.

A breeze rustles some leaves trapped in the hedge below them. Tim's hand, with smoke and a red glow between its fingers, indicates the surroundings. The street, the hedge, the night.

'I don't want to attribute all of this to a Creator. Why? I don't want to think anything is bigger than Life, or that Life was manufactured for some mysterious purpose that only gets revealed when we die. Like a sick flippin' gameshow. In't it more beautiful to think everything happened just because it did?'

But it doesn't seem beautiful to Oscar. To think nothing has a point, that things are only born to struggle and die. It's a side of Tim that makes him uneasy. They ought to change the subject.

'So you're not from here?'

'Hmm?' the man says, mid-smoke.

'You said West London. So you're not from here?'

'Oh. Well, no.' He seems disappointed, but then he covers it with a laugh. 'Couldn't you tell? I hail from t'Midlands, duck.' He exaggerates the accent.

'What's that— like, Derbyshire?'

'Watch yourself, son. I mean, yeah, Derby is Midlands, but I'm from Nottingham. We hate Derby.'

'Oh. Sorry.'

'Ah, you're alright. I'll just have to do the talking if we ever go there.'

There's a bite to the air. Charlotte's right, winter is peeking through. And Tim is suggesting they'll go to the Midlands together. To see his home. Nothing ever sounded more promising, even if the word 'Midlands' is an instant limp dick.

Alec's phone rings inside and he answers it, to his wife's muffled protests. Charlotte sounds lighter again, merry, and instructs her friend to leave the silly man to his business calls. The women laugh at something like schoolgirls passing notes while Alec makes himself heard around the neighbourhood. Xandra tries to shush him, but he ignores her.

It's album material. An album where all the music sounds like it's coming from another room. The singer's voice incredibly close, recorded on a phone in a wardrobe.

Tim doesn't seem to notice that there's another world going on indoors, but the sensation is an old acquaintance of Oscar's. The feeling of being a part of and apart from at the same time.

'Charlotte believes. In God.'

Tim, surprised for a moment, nods.

'Does it bother you?'

'No, of course not. Don't get me wrong,' he says, and turns to face him. 'Actually... OK, don't ever repeat this to anyone— But yeah, it does a bit. It annoys me when someone I like believes in God.'

Oscar's arms tingle, and something like a laugh escapes him. They'll be burned at the stake, thrown into rivers.

'I know,' Tim says, 'it makes me a total arse. Intolerant wanker, completely against my own "live and let live" ethos, but fuck it. I want all religions to die. Preferably before I do. I want to see a day when they don't even exist.'

The Eye is hidden inside Oscar's shirt, but Tim looks right at it. He's less than two feet away. His heart is also beating faster. He's going to lean in to Oscar, either kiss him or club him.

But the moment passes. He turns away again, drags on the cigarillo. Behind him, the moon looks flat as a penny.

'You might be right about tradition. Charlotte's parents, like— it sounds like they were religious.'

Tim slides the ashtray closer to Oscar. He acts casual, smoke billowing out of his mouth. 'Has she told you much about them?'

Charlotte has drip-fed info about her parents over the years. Mr Fontaine with his smart moustache. His interest in taxidermy, woodland creatures in particular. Mrs Fontaine's collection of recipes, the Mrs Beaton household manual. The page in the book that tells you where to seat the Archbishop and the Queen should they happen by for dinner. What a pair. Union flag in one hand, Bible in the other. Humbugs in their pockets, brown buckle shoes on their feet. Austerity Chic.

'She says they used to stand for *God Save the Queen*.'

Tim laughs, the shotgun laugh, and smokes. 'Join 'em or fight 'em,' he says. 'That's the illusion of choice, right?'

Probably?

'You either stand with your parents or against them, no choice but one of those.'

'Which are you? Like, what did you do?'

'Well,' he says, 'let's just say my old man would've voted UKIP if he were still alive. Can you believe it? Hated Thatcher, would've partied with the rest of us when she died, but there you go. Jump on the first fascist wagon that rattles by. Anyway, when I brought my first girlfriend home — she was this gorgeous lass called Lee, half-Thai. Petite, with these amazing green-gold eyes — and when my dad met her he actually said the words, and I'm not joking, "You're not one of them Chinks, are ya?"'

The shock of the impersonation subsides, and all that remains is *girlfriend, girlfriend, girlfriend*. It's so juvenile. Takes him back to school. The line of boys —even the OK ones — who felt the need to announce how straight they were around him. How much they liked tits, how tugging at another guy's shorts during rugby was part of the sport. It's the defence of many a guy, Lukas included. Make themselves attractive only to repel. Or repel in the hope that it makes them attractive. Spread their legs to kick you in the balls.

But Tim isn't like that. Not consciously. He must have an inkling of his effect on Oscar, must've caught a wistful glance at some point. But he's not the kind of man who would play a boy like that. Kick him when he's down. He's above that.

'So what did she say? Lee.'

Tim laughs with the smoke still in his mouth. He lets it out. 'She was pure class. She said, "Don't worry, I'm only half Chink." That shut him up.' Then he does it again. He looks at Oscar, lingers on his face. And no mistake, there's longing there.

Tim's shirtsleeves, rolled up to the elbow. The flesh of his arm goosepimpling in the cool breeze. The hairs. The need to stroke that arm, to warm those hairs into lying back down.

But he can't. That's Charlotte's duty. Her privilege.

Why does she get to get this? Why does she have to win? She's not that cultured, when all she's heard of is Dickens and Monet and *The Mikado*. Not that musical, when she's never moved beyond Tom Jones and Diana Ross. Not so smart, when her plots and characters have the depth of Cosmo. Not so pretty, with her shoulder-blades protruding and her skin betraying its vintage. The permanent brackets around her mouth. No amount of jogging and kale and Coelho can hide the fact that her youth is history. She writes mediocre novels for mediocre people. Her attitudes are dated. She's a touch xenophobic. She even believes in God.

Billie Holiday's voice comes scratching through his mind, from going-on-a-hundred years ago. *The Man I Love*. Heart on sleeve, heart in mouth.

He should say it, right now. *I like you*. Now that the two of them are alone together, and the others continue to talk inside. Before it's too late, *Tim, I like you*. It would be so simple, over so quick. The man's body is close. Just a mass of parts, a head at the tip, a chin to grab and turn, move towards his mouth, to say *I like you*. To kiss him.

'Oh,' Tim says, 'hang on.' He stubs out the smoke. 'I forgot to give you your present.'

And he puts a hand down his trouser pocket to pull out a gift, small as a pack of cards. Wrapped in brown paper, Austerity Chic.

'You're gonna think me such a cheapskate,' Tim says, 'or a complete and utter hipster. But whatever, I thought you'd get a kick out of it.'

The present, whatever it is, cannot be bad. He can't have got him a bad gift.

The paper tears easily. And when it falls, a mess on the balcony, all that remains in Oscar's hand is a tape. An actual cassette. A turn into the hipster cul-de-sac.

'It's a mixtape,' Tim says, cheeks going pink. As if he's made the biggest mistake and only just realised. 'Proper old-school, in't it?'

It is a mistake. A big, big mistake.

'I'm sorry I didn't write the track-list on there, either. What a bell-end.'

'No…'

He should finish the sentence, but no other words will come. Tim's mistake was big enough to shut him up.

And there's the silver lining.

I like you. Shut up.

On their tenth anniversary, Charlotte gave Oscar a record player. It came in its own red leather case, so all she had to do was stick a bow on it and sing with a quiver in her voice as she presented it. *Happy birthday to you…* And when she pulled out a separate case of seven-inch vinyls, his jaw dropped almost totally off his head. Fauxhemian douche. Practically fitting as he unclasped the gold locks and let the red leather case creak open. As he stroked that turntable and the volume knobs, and ran a finger over the tops of all those singles boxed together…

It was more than a gift Charlotte had given him. It was a rite of passage. The equivalent of sending him to a Jamaican whorehouse to become a man, and he was thankful for it. Marvin Gaye and Sarah Vaughn popped his cherry. Dinah Washington, Nina Simone, Otis Redding, Patsy Kline, Julie London, John Lee Hooker, Etta James.

Oscar spent the rest of that year in his bedroom, pumping songs about grapevines and backwater blues and smoking in bed and grandma's hands through his ears. When he got an iPhone for the eighth anniversary, the love was purely physical.

Now in his palm sits a long-dead form of gift, so dead it could've belonged to the Brontës. A mixtape. Not a CD, not a Spotify playlist. A mixtape, made for mysterious reasons by a man who came into his life by falling into Charlotte's.

Tim is courting him. Surely he must know that no matter what the tape contains, it's going to be judged as a piece of art. Something with an agenda, to decode and analyse. If this isn't romance, nothing is.

Charlotte still has a tape player, on which she records her novels and plays them back for editing. Its little blue bulb is the only source of light in Oscar's bedroom. The curtains are drawn. Darkness brings focus.

The tape crackles, and the first song begins. A sax. A sudden swoop of male voices, like a crooked chant. A faded piano, bass and the grinding sax. The elements join together in a sexy strut, and a man's voice rises out of the trip. He sings of a lusty booze-joint in Mexico. Hot drinks, hot staff. What happens when you cross that border. *Down in Mexico*.

The Mayfairs wither in Oscar's mouth. The little fire-bucket ashtray Bella got him last Christmas fills to the brim with ash. A minute more of this tape and the whole cursed flat will be burned to the ground.

He and Tim in Mexico, or a country like it. Somewhere with markets, and Disney-eyed, suntanned kids playing cards on doorsteps. Hanging fabrics, spice in the air and a sun without mercy. Tim's hand on his back — or walking slightly ahead, holding him by the hand — guiding him through the crowd. His shirt hanging open, the taut body beneath it, the physique of a tennis player. In a sweat. At a bar, or sitting outside a coffee shop, facing the street, or in the hotel room. Tim lying back on the bed, pulling Oscar with him, peeling off his own shirt so that his slick back sticks to the sheets. Oscar's hand sliding down from Tim's chest, carving a path through the hairs on his body, down to the zip on his jeans.

There's some stuff on the tape he's already acquainted with. Savages and Dylan. That song by Girls, with the gospel singer's voice towering over the musical chaos as the lead searches for love...

By the time the last song steps out through the tape noise, some sixty minutes later, Oscar's lungs are caked in tar.

Then a familiar voice, full of pain. The sheer life of it. Jacques Brel.

Ne me quitte pas.

It's more than a coincidence.

Tim knows.

The Eye is in his hand again, both a shield and a birthday candle. A prayer goes 'round in Oscar's head, veering between two desires — love, and protection against it.

What does Tim mean by all this? How can he put together a mixtape and not expect Oscar to pan it for gold? How did he know what songs to use on him? Was he in this room, searching for clues? Sitting on this bed?

No. He simply knew.

The craving grows inside him. To belong to someone, and them belong to you. To have the licence to touch him when the mood takes you. An affectionate hand on his cheek, or his thigh. To be able to see him at the sink, brushing his teeth, shaving, or sitting at his desk, and put your arms around him, bring him closer. To look down at the top of his head on your chest, the spiral of thousands of hairs. Or to feel his chest against your head, his heartbeat in your ears. To thread your fingers through his as you wander through the city. To know this person exists and that you have each other. That you were drawn to each other. That you're just two bodies drifting through an ancient world.

The guys who stand outside the bars of Soho fade into the ground. Bits of newspaper pressed into the pavement by a city of shoes. Faded to ghosts in the concrete, in the rain and The Big Smoke. Tattoo transfers. Tim is more than a million of them put together. A solid man. Everything's easy with him, they have a dialect in common. When he's around, the world is a better place.

There's no way Charlotte can claim him.

There are moments when being with Tim feels attainable. Not a mere desire, but a peek at the future. But there follows the dread that it's only a fiction. An embarrassing fantasy. Those lips are out of bounds, love beyond Oscar's reach. Like that time he was the only sober person at a New Year's Eve party (nobody noticed), and a coked-out girl with long red hair slid the French windows open, ran to chase the fireworks over Hampstead

Heath. They all ran after her, the less impaired, but she still reached through that tangle of arms towards the sky.

'He wants Charlotte.'

There's something between them.

Tim is straight.

'But I want him.'

Shut up.

'I want him.'

Keep chasing fireworks.

'I want him.'

Get a God.

07 ON YOUR SIDE

There's been no visit from the man in days, and Charlotte's been more cautious with her conversation. When she moves her legs on the sofa for Oscar to sit down next to her, a ticker-tape of thoughts runs across her face before she opens her mouth. But the things she leaves unsaid are still heard. Messages, non-verbal signals, from one body to another. When she places her hand on Oscar's knee, when she makes his bed and unfurls a blanket over the duvet, when she picks out fluff or fallen bits of leaves from his hair and holds V-neck jumpers up to his torso, when she sits on the sofa sipping tea and blushing at a text on her phone, Charlotte is announcing, *I'm with Tim, I'm with Tim.*

But it can't be. He's too young for her. Then again, there must be the same number of years between Charlotte and Tim as Tim and Oscar. In both equations, one of them's a toy boy.

It's been so long since Oscar last got laid, they probably do things differently now. Terry was his first and last. That night they went back to his place, the flat his parents had bought him on Berkeley Square, and fumbled with trembling fingers. First on the sofa, then on his bed.

And Charlotte. Writing all her dirty thoughts in those journals, to be published for a wide readership. Hot young men in loose white shirts. Older women with a thing for lace. Leather and belt buckles. Rose petals on naked skin.

Now she's caught one for herself, a handsome tin soldier. Why else would Tim have come to the flat as often as he has? Literary house calls cannot be in his job description.

When a couple of pieces fall into place, the others come in quick succession. Xandra controlled herself that night at Claridge's, when the men were debating — she who's been known to shoot down waiters over over-browned pastry — because Tim is special to Charlotte. When Xandra visits, whispers in tears in the kitchen about Alec, his pretty assistants and the charges on his credit card bills, Charlotte's is the calming voice in the kitchen. The friend putting the kettle on, the woman unburdened by a husband.

Whenever she mentions Tim, her casualness reeks of rehearsal. She doesn't want Oscar to know, which means she knows it would upset him. Her fake son is not OK, and she's aware of it. There's no way he'll be OK if she carries on like this. She knows it. And yet she's still doing it.

This is a woman who has given him her home, the lioness' share of her food. She has clothed and protected him, kept him out of the gutter and away from the food banks. She's been a mother. What more can he want? And she's a far cry from Bella's mum, the barrister who calls her daughter to lunch in Aldwych, who tries again and again to convince the unemployed History graduate to take the Bar. She can't see that her brand of caring only cripples a child. Charlotte is careful not to be them, the parents she never had and never would be. She has no plans for him, no ambitions other than to sit right there and be loved. Be loved, God damn you. Because he only has basic needs — hunger, warmth, affection — that she fulfils. Everything else is illusion.

The headphones are back on his head, having been found by Carolina in a jacket about to join the Salvation Army. Shuffle's on and Marvin Gaye is playing, *Got To Give It Up*. Showing the newbies how it's done.

The track does the Hustle around his eardrums, but Oscar's mind drifts to a different tune. One heading south of the border, down to Mexico.

The sax intermingles with the disco beat, Marv's falsetto overlaid with the other man's yearning, whoever he was, whoever his gang of boys chanting behind him were. The bongos, the castanets. Marvin's bassline, his falsetto.

The beat shimmies down Oscar's legs, makes them twitch. One, then the other. And when his hip starts moving, it brings the spinal column, and his head, with it.

Bassline. A spicy waitress.

Different bassline. Bell-bottoms and afros.

It's like Tokyo on the train carriage — People are pretending not to look. The tourists and the chick with the hoop earrings popping gum in her mouth. Basic bitch. When Marvin's over, The Weeknd comes in. His languid rap, the ice-cold synth. Nothing makes a white guy whiter than hip-hop leaking out of his headphones. Gum Girl is staring. *Cracker,* she's thinking. But dancing is universal, eternal. Harks back to the Stone Age.

Charlotte hates rap. She finds it all offensive, from the rhythm to the content she assumes is there. She probably wonders why black artists are no longer Tamla. Tim will see all of this in her soon, if he hasn't already.

The tube stops. People get off, chattering, taking their H&M bags and paperbacks. An old lady climbs on board, and she is bringing her A-game. Lipstick the colour of sunburn, matching hat and coat and heels, Youth Dew shooting forth. These old folks grew up here, their lives entangled with the city's. Taking cover underground when the place was being blitzed by the Nazis, phoning grandkids as soon as the first Seventh of July bomb broke the news. Not even the threat of Daesh keeps them from living. Tories and Labour, Thatcher and Blair, Diana and Kate, protests and London Pride, everything seen and done already. Charlotte is just as much a product of this place as them, London as much a part of her.

But Tim isn't a product of it. And since at one point in time an accent betrayed his background, it's safe for Oscar to assume that he isn't either.

When the music stops, the silence between the tracks allows the commuter noise to drip through. A beggar's giving his speech to the carriage, about how he only needs a few pounds for the shelter tonight. Some folks look annoyed, others drop coins in his cup. Then there are snippets of conversation — *Really need a sugar thermometer* — before the next tune starts in Oscar's ears.

Whatever it is. It's not the one that's making him dance.

Maya's schmoozing with her guests, pointing out the features of her new flatshare. After years of flirting with the concept, she's finally gone full Bohemian, moved into a converted hospital, somewhere formerly deprived. In a part of London where boys dress like Velma from *Scooby-Doo* and sit at cafés selling milkshakes and bike bells in one swoop. Not far from here, Maya pimps her handmade jewellery in an indie boutique, attends magazine launches in former breweries.

Lukas is across the room, downing a Red Stripe with a random. His jaw is moving while his mouth is shut. Always finding something to chew. Bella stares at him when she thinks no-one's looking. When she turns to catch Oscar's eye, she adopts an expression of fatigue, as if the party and its denizens are wearing her out.

Maya came over to them earlier on, half-asleep, hair changed from braids into old-school afro and lips a hot wet pink. She told them she loved them, and Bella thanked her. She touched Oscar's cheek, and mouthed it again.

Two hours, Rihanna, Jay-Z and a few shots later, Oscar and Bella are motionless but breathing, two sets of heartbeats on the sofa. The cushions are plump and threadbare, bought from a British Heart Foundation as if Maya were as broke as her flatmates. Bella's head rests on Oscar's chest, her hair in his nose as she sighs. Kanye West thumping the entire room — *blood on the leaves* — and the table's laid thick with houmous and breadsticks, salt-coated vegetable crisps, Kopparbergs, traces of coke and ashtrays full of buds. Bella's ribcage vibrates against his. She's laughing. Lazily, at nothing, but still. It makes him smile. If she wasn't drunk, she wouldn't even be resting against him, let alone laughing through his body.

Lukas finally swaggers over to join them. 'Hey, you two lovebirds!' he says. His jeans are so low it's only a wispy layer between his pubes and the room.

Bella lifts her head. 'Lukas, what the fuck is that?'

Clipped to his T-shirt is a ceramic white poppy. He looks down at it. 'What? You mean this? It's a poppy, genius. Sammy got it for me.'

'That isn't a poppy.'

'Yeah it is. It's white because it represents peace?'

She's facing away from him but Bella's mood could freeze bones. She lowers her head onto Oscar's chest, heavy. 'Oh my God,' she murmurs. 'You can be such an arse.'

Lukas is taken aback. Those moving grey irises, scanning for sarcasm. But, as usual, Bella's attack seems not to have wounded him. He crashlands on the sofa next to them, makes it dip. That bottle of Red Stripe at his mouth. Beer on his lips, along with peanuts, and anything else that's been there in the past few hours. Joints. Tits. Protein shakes. Salmon.

Bella's eyelashes flutter against Oscar's shirt. She'll remember the white poppy business tomorrow, a storm still brewing. Don't ask him about country capitals, Ayatollahs or rebel groups, or what the hell a Shadow Secretary is, but show him a poster of a soldier's widow and Oscar's wallet falls open. When Bella spots an ad like that, she scowls. The air around her bristles, and the closer she gets to the posters the quicker his heart beats with the fear that this time, she might just go ahead and do something.

It's a good thing there's no conscription these days, 'cause Oscar would be useless to Her Majesty. Too scared and disgusted by battle even to write poetry for kids to recite in school. If extremists or Putin or Korea start a war, and he were sent to the front, he'd fall arse-over-tit beneath the nearest marine and wait until it all blew over. But better to be blown to bits, annihilated, than coming home partly broken. Legs blown off. Putting your limbs on before your trousers.

'So where's your Norwegian?' Lukas says.

It had never even occurred to Oscar to ask her. To his surprise, Lukas is frowning. Makes his eyes look hard.

Bella thinks before she speaks. 'It wasn't to be.'

She lowers her head onto Oscar again, hugging herself, the long sleeves hiding her hands.

'Wow,' Lukas says, 'that was quick.'

She doesn't reply.

Lukas mouths to Oscar above her head, *Is she OK?*

If Oscar had a clue, he would say. Lukas turns away, giving up. He looks more annoyed with Bella than sorry for insulting her. After a minute, he rises from the sofa, the shift moving their lifeless bodies. He leaves the lost causes to themselves.

Another two hours have ebbed, and the same breezy dance-pop track has been playing for what seems like hours. A group of couples sits around two guys in checked shirts playing Connect 4.

Girls sit drowsy on their boyfriends' knees. 'When I was in Amsterdam, they smoked their weed completely pure?'

Two chicks fall from the sofa, leggings, leggings without skirts, pissing themselves.

'... taught English in Vietnam. So cheap over there.'

'Obviously, I'm twenty-four, and I've just come to the point in my life —'

A ginger beard and a deep voice, a bunch of other guys around him. 'Chopped his fucking head off!'

'Yeah-yeah-yeah,' laughing.

Shirt so tight it's like paint on his pecs. Gay.

'Top-quality pressing.' Dude wears a beanie on the tip of his scalp like it's a Yarmulke. Beardy guys in bands. Ramshackle fucking indie.

A girl with turquoise curls. 'I did one that was basically slavery.'

Stripy scarf, ballet shoes.

'You need a PGCE.'

No, *you* need a PGCE.

Moustaches sprouting on faces. Must be Movember.

A fine slab of man. What the Yanks would call a jock. Rugby shirt, notes of beer and Lynx on his man-size frame. He'll quote *Family Guy*, damn, even as he rams you into a headboard. He and his pals get off when they're drunk. How far do they go before one of them cries chicken?

It's been months since he was touched.

'I don't get why they wanted to split from us, like, what's the point?'

Another girl, sipping a Bacardi Breezer with her ears cocked, she's just nice. Maggie Smith eyelids and a snowman's chin. Why would you feel sad for her? Who for?

Why are you taking five-hundred photos of the turbaned man? said an old flame, on the grounds of the Crystal Palace ruins.

Because the statue survived a fire, and everything around him crumbled. Because he's looking out at the few remaining stones, and the hill and the city below. Because he can't talk.

His eyes are moist. It's hot in here.

Who wants Facebook and Twitter, Instagram or Tumblr? Who cares what you ate, or photographed eating, or even how you feel? What does it matter?

GAME OF THRONES FINALE!!!

Stay in the EU!

Fake news.

BRITAIN FIRST.

Rugby Guy is staring.

The ghost of a melody comes to him. Smells of smoke. He'll grab his throat when he cuts the vocals, fuck it up somehow. Toast, peanut butter.

Say the word, dude.

Too American.

Say the word. When and where? When and where, Rugby Shirt?

As though he'd ever. Guy's not all that. Buff body with a plasticine face. Bell-end. He'd pour a pint over two chicks at once and lick it off.

Slap me.

Too much. How do you know he's rough like that?

Because you know. Because he has no lips and the veins rise out of the crook of his arm.

When and where, Rugby Shirt?

His head is filled. His throat is dry, heart worn out from beating. The corridor is lined with people, their hands moving over each other.

I like you.

Ever since you told me that story. With the Eye.

'... residency at the BAC.'

You're the first thing in my brain when I wake up. The last when it shuts down.

I like you.

'... she shoved it in James' face.'

Obviously, I don't expect anything to happen— I mean, you're with Charlotte.

'Mate — squats. No word of a lie.'

But I want you to know.... You mean something to somebody.

'... did fifteen reps.'

To me. Me.

'Five-nil.'

I like you.

Rugby Shirt's face in front of his. The guy looks confused, his eyebrows knitted. 'What the fuck ... ?' And his friends surround them, laughing and braying. 'Wanker,' they say, and, 'Oh, jokes! Thicky's got a boyfriend!'

Oscar's hands are on the Rugby Shirt. His chest is harder than Terry's. More meat to fill his hands.

'Get off me, you ginger fuck!' Rugby Shirt says.

But it's all so funny. What's he upset about?

Why?

'Because I'll fucking deck you, that's why.'

The guy wants it, it's clear. If they keep going like this, he'll give in. A game of Chicken taken all the way. 'Kiss me.'

The other guys whoop and cheer. Lukas and Maya rush towards him.

Kiss me.

And when his face is pressed up against the other, a spark, but Rugby Shirt leans back, not afraid, but with purpose, to bring his forehead slamming back like a catapult. It knocks Oscar to the floor, his back and shoulders landing on other people's feet. Lukas and Maya yell at the guy, Maya telling him to leave. And a bunch of men point at the boy on the floor, laughing at the spectacle.

The bathroom door is unlocked, whines open at a touch. Bella's in a heap by the terracotta toilet, eyes red and wet. One of the flatmates' blue damp towels is hanging from the rack and brushing her shoulder. When she sees him, her mouth breaks into a smile.

'I'm a hot mess, Oskovich,' she says. Mouth twisting to laugh. 'I hate everything.' She pulls him down to the floor with her, against the damp heat of the towel on the radiator. 'I have so much energy for hating everything.' Her head falls onto his chest again, sniffs into his T-shirt.

'I like you.'

She looks up, wiping her eyes. 'What … ?'

'I like you.'

In a split second, she sobers up. She's staring hard at his eyes. No emotion, just science. 'Oh Christ, Osky… Who did this? Are you all right?' She gently touches his face, then gets up to wet a small towel under the tap and press it to the bone above his eye. If only he could bring himself to speak of Tim, to share the truth with her, this silent barrier could be lifted. Life would be a gas. She'd speak up too. She'd admit that the date with the Norwegian was a mistake. Or a total fabrication. Or that an older geek with a paunch is the only type of man she could ever face undressing for.

Fifteen minutes later, they're outside on the fire escape, a bonfire raging in the courtyard below. The Guy's been burnt to cinders already. A girl unknown to both of them says they burned an effigy of Alex Salmond in Lewes. Whoever that is, wherever that is.

Lukas stands at his other side, won't leave him alone since Rugby Shirt's head-butt. The flames flicker on his face, on the faces all around, and for a minute everyone's silent. The buff lads, the girls in tutus and boots, the gamers. It's like everyone's remembering something, something sweet and long gone.

It comes to him in fragments. Phrases and inflections, a little colour, a little shading, in those moments when his room is dark, and the duvet a ghost in the moonlight, when sleep feels both imminent and far away. The fantasy takes place in Charlotte's sitting room, or a version of it — one lacking in detail, but essentially it. They sit facing each other, Tim in the armchair and Oscar on the settee. Tim has that half-perplexed, half-amused look on his face, same as when he's trying to think of an answer to a question. In the fantasy, Oscar clears his throat. He leans forward like a man and moves his hands with restraint. He's never been so straight in his life.

Tim, he says, *I've got to tell you something. And it's something you probably already know, but that doesn't make it any easier. Look, you came suddenly into our lives — my life — and I'm normally the sort of person that things just happen to. And you happened to me. Your stories and your… effect. It happened to me. And I'm glad it did. Ever since the book launch, you've intrigued me. But my feelings sort of… developed from there. I like you, Tim. I know, it's wrong and I shouldn't — you're in love with Charlotte, and she's like my mum, so… yeah. So I don't expect anything to happen. I only wanted to tell you, so you know. That somebody else cares for you. You're the first thought in someone's head in the morning, the last one at night. You matter to someone. You happened to him and he's glad you did.*

The smoke from Tim's cigarillo fills the space between them. The air is charged. Tim's eyes have narrowed and his smile has faded. He leans forward and exhales. *How long have you felt this way?* A glimmer in his eye.

Ever since you told me about the Eye and that old woman in Greece. I wanted to kiss you then. So badly.

Tim leans even further forward until his smoke gets in Oscar's eyes. It travels through his nose and rubs its way around his head.

And they kiss.

No tongues, no reckless passion. Only a joining of lips. The simple proof that someone's on your side, and that he likes you back.

08 MEAT

There's half a bird on the train track. A fist of feathers, hard to distinguish from the pebbles and stones, and a single foot stretched over a wooden panel. Birds aren't as fragile as they look. They're beasts, with thick curling talons, like those hawks they bring to Trafalgar Square, with men in thick leather gauntlets, to frighten the pigeons away. More feathers, floating off along the track. The beak must be around here somewhere.

A man in a too-small suit is staring at it, too. His shirt cuffs poke too far out of his jacket sleeves, and the knot of his tie is anaemic. As if he was forced to dress for a wedding by his mother, when all he wanted was to climb a tree. Charlotte, Kiehl's bag swinging from her wrist, threads her arm through Oscar's. They're the same height. He once thought he'd outgrow her, but they've managed to stay in sync, like women on their period. They're stuck together for ever. Like Big and Little Edie of Grey Gardens, Blanche and Baby Jane. They'll live in a ransacked mansion eating soup made from home-grown leeks and fighting over the last remaining postman.

When the train comes, it'll run the bird over again. It's not like the driver could stop in time, or swerve to avoid it. A driver stopping an entire train — the whole huge mass of it slamming into itself, inertia piling onto it from behind. Is that what inertia is? As a kid, he pictured a big fat lady in a floral dress tumbling down a stairwell.

There's an Arab guy on the platform, so massive you can see his pecs through the navy gilet. In a body like that, the tangle of organs and blood seems possible. But Charlotte is so wispy in comparison, made of miniature lungs and the flimsiest cartilages. Her narrow shoulders. Small as that half of a bird on the track.

The moment she laid eyes on him that morning at breakfast, she insisted on rushing him to A&E. Spent the whole of the cab journey thanking God he'd survived the night. The whitecoats took a long look and concluded Rugby Shirt's head-butt had done no serious damage. There was definite swelling, and some mild bruising that turned ugly until it was beautiful. *Jolie laide*. Best thing his A-level art teacher ever taught him, that aberrations could be pretty. That a moth's tongue is both creepy and a wondrous spiral. The burst of melanin on his face, the stormy purple and the luminescent green, so unreal yet totally real, on his forehead, over the skull over the brain — it's ugly-pretty. The pain that shoots through it when touched. The mere thought of the nerves and muscle... The thought that if Rugby Shirt's head-butt, even later, all of a sudden in the middle of the night, might've ended his life...

It's kept him shut in his room for days, the mixtape on loop. The moment he got the news from Charlotte, Tim sent a text to wish him better, but the days have ticked by since then, and the man's absence is a cold hard stone. He's not avoiding Oscar, he's just busy at the office. Negotiating in French and Spanish about rights and translations. Finding clients, making money, living his life. Keeping a distance.

All he has to do is come back, or at the very least text again, and all will be alright. But, of course, he doesn't.

The general readings on the horoscope app are vague enough to give Oscar hope. It's nobody's fault if Jupiter's in retrograde, or Venus and Pluto aren't aligned. Sometimes, things are in ascendant. And of course that affects things.

Tim is a body, just a body, who was born to get old and die.

But even thoughts of him in thirty years' time do nothing to diminish his impact. Older Tim is present in the young one. His future brow, his worn skin, the faint haggardness of the stressed-out agent. His future widow's peak, every time his hand runs through his hair. His future belly, when he stretches and yawns without covering his mouth, and his shirt and jumper pull away from his chinos. The brown hairs of that belly, waiting to turn grey. Tim in a cardigan, reading in his favourite armchair. Making a stir-fry, playing Captain Beefheart and singing along, not badly but not well either. It could be so.

Except it won't be, because the fantasy excludes Oscar. Somewhere along the way, they've dropped out of each other's lives. They're doomed. They don't get to become those old gents sitting side-by-side on the Central line for Notting Hill, leaning in for a chaste kiss.

That's where the fault lies — a brain lesion. Maybe Rugby Shirt knocked it out, knocked some sense into him. There's only ever been one of them in the dream. The other is resigned to dreaming.

Tim is straight. Incapable of feeling for Oscar what Oscar is incapable of stopping.

The bruise on his forehead worsens, then fades. But it's all still going on under there, a chemical war under his skin.

Jolie laide.

Once outside the station, Bella dodges Jehovah's Witnesses and charity fundraisers to lead the way along the tree-lined street. She tells him it's time for the Hunterian, which sounds like a folk dance or a *Doctor Who* monster. Turns out it's a museum, huge stone pillars across from a tennis pitch empty of players. Inside, the place is all marble and security guard, a front desk at which Bella procures visitor tags from a woman with no lips, such is her lack of time for this shit. Bella leads him upstairs, spewing facts about the building and the statue where someone's ashes are kept, a husband and wife and her lover, but it's all too quick for Oscar to process. He should take himself down to Foyles or a library, to the Popular Science bays. History

& Politics. Learn something, get an education that doesn't revolve around artists who drowned themselves in lakes.

Today, at least, there is biology. A watering hole for hypochondriacs. An entire room, two floors, full of glass cases. Jars of specimens reaching up to the ceiling, the top few rows impossible to see from his vantage point. Bella points out shark embryos, rat embryos, kangaroos and cats, spleens, disembodied hands and feet, nipples, ulcers and, *pièce de resistance*, a syphilitic knob.

It saddens Oscar to see a penis parted from its owner. Even if it did take a few minutes for the wang, hidden within that shapeless mass in the jar, to become clear.

'What do you call this?'

'A damn shame, Osky.'

'No, the liquid they put it in.'

'Oh. Uh… formaldehyde? Hey, come see this.'

She's hunched over an eyepiece, flicking through slides. Photos of plastic surgery's early days. She says it's nothing you don't see on *Embarrassing Bodies*. But the thought of Great War survivors' ravaged faces, after a bunch of Frankensteins have fucked around with them, makes him queasy. It was bad enough seeing one half of a child's face earlier. Followed by half a monkey's. Nicer to think of ceramic poppies, spilling out of the Tower, and wonder how long he's got left to see them before they go.

Part of him wants to flick through the slides. To become desensitised, and react to the faces of the brave dashing fighters and the pulp beneath their skin with detachment. But he just isn't man enough.

The dick in the jar, on the other hand — that's astonishing. It once belonged to someone, apparently served him well. It was once attached to a pelvic whatever, hundreds of years ago, 'til it succumbed to illness, and its owner to death, and a doctor's formaldehyde. Now it sits in a jar, to people's horror and delight. He should text Tim about it, bring him here. They'd marvel at this whole place together. If Tim hasn't seen it already. It would make the man smile to receive a text, saying,

Standing in front of a 200-year-old dick in a jar. Lesson of the day — always wear a condom.

Might even make him blush. Make him link the thought of sex with the thought of Oscar. Connotations are the smart man's army.

On Gower Street, a Latin-looking buck jogs by in cycling shorts. 'He looks a right handful,' Bella says with a smirk. 'I want to be *very* nice to him.' She arches her brows but there's no smile to be got from Oscar. A few months ago, he'd have cackled, and they'd have spent the rest of the afternoon watching prime cuts of beef strut around Soho Square. Bella would bemoan everyone's gayness, curse Oscar for his fortune. Inevitably some muscle-daddy would size him up. His body used to work a kind of magic, pheromones or something, to lasso the men on the street with. Now something's gone, left him sexless. These days, a pair of Lycra shorts is tinged with bitterness. Are they uncomfortable? Does the man have trouble on public transport, or watching plays in old theatres? Is he an attention-whore, spread all over Brighton and Snapchat and Grindr? There's no enjoyment to be had at the sight of a decent package these days, only analysis.

i. Two testes and a penis.
ii. Tubes and blood cells.
iii. Tumescence occurs.

It's a fucking annotated diagram, so intimate it's miles away.

The buck in the Lycra shorts stops for a breather, stretches. Bella walks backwards to watch, doesn't blink for eight minutes. She pretends to feel faint, wafts some air to her face with a dainty hand. 'Oh, I say!' she whispers.

Her ear sticks out from under her woolly hat. It juts out from her skull, and she underlines the flaw by pushing a strand of hair back behind it. Charlotte would think they spoiled her looks, those jutting ears. If they ever met.

The jogger has a handsome face. A Roman statue's nose and a cleft chin. Square, stubbled jaw. Chestnut curls on top. Puts Tim to shame.

But there's nothing. Not even a stirring in Oscar's belly. Not dim admiration, not envy and definitely not lust. The beautiful man is there and he exists. That's all.

—•—

A schoolgirl got caught in a crossfire in Deptford. Two boys were arrested, but there are more gangs out there, hundreds, according to the Metros people read around him on the tube. The girl died quickly, riddled with bullets. That's the hope, anyhow. That the metal shot through her brain first, put the lights out. It made the killers laugh, to see her shut-down body collapse on itself and fall to the ground. The same event made a boy laugh and a mother cry. That girl, once alive and now not. How bleak that she doesn't get to be revived, to walk home with Jesus.

Tim has a point. There's a comfort in viewing feelings scientifically, even if science evokes sombre nerds and Petri dishes. It helps to see emotions as responses to stimuli. Alerts to the nervous system. Composers crank out the strings to make you get out the Kleenex. A pedalled piano chord, minor key, reverbs through the bones and turns them to jelly. Straight-up science.

It's not heartache that Tim isn't here. It's only that his presence in the room makes Oscar feel good, because he says things that are good to hear, in a pitch and timbre that float Oscar's boat, and because his features are shapes that, through a long string of reactions, have been linked to pleasure. When Tim leaves the room, there's an absence of pleasure. The further away he is, the bigger the lack. Simple deprivation, of all the things that mix your chemicals, make you process as joy in what they tell you is your heart. The stimuli for these reactions are out there, gathered together in a single body, a mass of nerves and chemicals, that can be broken down into atoms, and protons, electrons, and whatever else that sounds like a wizard from *The Hobbit*.

We begin as blood. It was in a documentary Charlotte caught on BBC4 one night. The gravel-voiced presenter cut into a fertilised chicken egg with a flick-knife, coaxed a bit of shell away to reveal a fresh new heart. The opening note. A little red pool with streams stemming from it. Nothing as sublime as a Soul. Only a being. A random composition.

But that is sublime, goddamn it. That guy sitting opposite him with a face like a brick, he's only atoms. Those glaring eyes are only millions and millions of parts of a whole. If he slammed a fistful of them into Oscar's face, he'd have punched the atoms out of him. They'd mingle with the atoms all around until he became unified with the retro-mauve carpet seats of the Metropolitan line, and that Indian lady with the gaping mouth. And that lady 'chose' to wear pink trainers and a sun visor through a series of neurological responses, as opposed to the will of a vengeful God.

Xandra made an offhand comment about liver spots once. They don't just appear, she said, but have been there all along. Her doctor told her. They get revealed, when we're older and weaker and the fat beneath our skins has melted who-knows-why-or-where-to. It's a thought that's haunted Oscar, filled him with fear and amazement at the body's talents. Like when you're a teenager and someone says 'spontaneous combustion' in the school canteen. Baked beans fall out of mouths, potato jackets harden.

What do you mean, like, you can just explode? No warning?

Yeah, literally, something happens and your body overheats like an old pipe and you pop like a balloon.

There's a tragicomic romance in that. Something a bit sad and hilarious at the same time, to die working up a sweat to *Single Ladies* on the dancefloor, leaving behind a pair of knee-high rhinestone boots and a patch of Topshop denim.

Screw Tim. He needs to learn to text. And come over again. However busy he is, if he wanted to he'd make the time.

Charlotte can have him. She can vape and write and sign books for fans and roll under Tim.

Oscar is a guy, and guys are supposed to have needs. Tim is not fulfilling them. Tim is nobody.

A body. No more.

Cold turkey hasn't worked. It's brought him to Soho, the streets black as oil and iced as Coke. A rickshaw driver dings his bell to chase pedestrians off the road, Oscar included. Turning a corner brings him face to face with a horse, dusty white, next to which is a chocolate mate. The mounted cops lead the beasts in the direction of Piccadilly, the clop of their hooves reminding Oscar of the frailty of bones. His feet take him away.

People everywhere. Friends and colleagues having after-work drinks. East-Asian girls in doorways, backpackers declining the invite. Men and boys on the prowl, picking Oscar out in the pink and green lights of clubs and bars like a fox among the bins.

Lights in a patisserie window — *vitrine* — turn the place into a gingerbread house. The profiteroles, éclairs, glazed fruit tartlets, marzipan pears and chocolate truffles on display. The laminated menus on the door. The wine selection, the hot beverages. Customers perusing the selection up-close inside, looking up to chat, looking down to choose, not actually registering anything but talking and smiling, apologising to the staff for taking so long to decide. There are tables of ladies who lunched, and there are tables of lonely souls, whether readers or businessmen or drag queens with dogs in Fendi handbags. A waiter points him out to a colleague. They wave, thinking him insane or homeless or both.

On the other side of the street, there's a crowd of gays standing together. They drink, chat, side-eye, laugh. One of them talks in that tone of voice his mother must've gossiped with. It puts Oscar on edge, the thought of what might be said about him if these peers ever noticed him. Even among his supposed people, he's only ginger and skinny and fostered. Some guys go for that, maybe for all of the above, but it's not worth the pain to look for them. Not now, at this messy stage. Christ.

No — not Christ. There's nothing Biblical about any of this. There was no King James and there was no Milton when two guys first looked across the campfire at each other and extended their fingers to touch. But if you can't mention your gayness to a Christian or a Muslim or a B&B owner for fear of being imprisoned, 'cured', beheaded or dismissed, you should at least feel safe amongst others of your kind.

But nobody's of his kind.

But Tim.

Rain, thank fuck. Come to wash this man right out of his hair.

A young waif stands by a streetlamp. At first it looked like the boy from the DLR, the drunk who wouldn't keep his hands to himself. Bumping into the same stranger twice would be far too much of a coincidence. But not impossible. What's eight million people, in the grand scheme of things? He should've accepted Drunk Boy's invitation when he had the chance. There'd be nothing wrong with a bit of nameless sex, as long as they were careful. Everyone's an outsider, a stranger to everyone else. Should've slept with the boy when the opportunity presented itself, got his fix and given him his. The prude. The chances of finding the boy now, and of the boy being as drunk, or as willing...

This waif on the corner is all ankle boots and skinny jeans. A Calvin-Kleined arse peeks above the waistband, a flimsy vest shows off the T of his sculpted tits. The smooth brown skin. The earring sparkling at his ear. He walks away, his back to Oscar, attracting him. It makes no sense, boy's a twink. Oscar can't want this.

Empty plastic bags scuttle across the streets like animals. The voices of men and women clatter out of pubs. Cabs try to push through the crowds walking to and fro in the road, thigh-high boots, heels, sneakers and brogues. Beefy lads and skinny boys. Massage parlours. Sex shops, with mannequins stretching in crotchless lycra. Arseless leather.

Finally, the twink walks into a club. The UV lights and music, repetitive, nameless, pull Oscar right in after him.

Boys at the bar, buying each other drinks. Men in threes doing shots. The bassline pounds through his feet, chatter and synth blend together. Blonds in tight shirts, brunettes with buckles the size of their fists. A guy licks tongues with a man in a tweed waistcoat. A silver hoop stretching out his earlobe, big enough to fit a wrist. Another guy looks way out of place, holding his cocktail and watching the crowd. A patch of fluffy brown hair high up on his forehead, eyes of Isaac Newton. Every time a head swivels away from the guy, Oscar's heart aches. As though the poor thing doesn't know the others are too hot for him, beings on a higher level. They know a dozen different ways to work their abs, have a favourite brand of protein shake. Loaded with whey or brown rice, or whatever it is that adds meat to a chest.

There's got to be a state other than sitting in corners, watching the hotties pass by. A parallel world where the tables are turned. Beautiful people know no other way of living. Never have to dream of being sexy, of leaving a line of stunned admirers in their wake. All those skipped heartbeats, blanching the air…

One of that demigod breed is on the dancefloor. He stands out from the crowd, a red-headed statue. A figure from da Vinci's sketchbooks. Moving, writhing.

A slim older man in a violet shirt stares at Oscar. He makes his way over to take him by the hand, unblinking. He leads them through the dancing bodies as if they're children crossing a field, and his earrings sparkle as he starts to gyrate against him. The demigod has vanished. Glimpses of his head appear, now and again, above and through the other heads, the happy, the horny, the lonely. One of them looks high as a surfer, poking the air with his finger in tiny, constricted movements. A couple of straight girls dance with each other, laughing, hair swaying with their backs.

Then the redhead comes up again. He's Oscar in a parallel world. His vest clings to his torso, soaks up the sweat, stretches against him. The DJ mixes in another track. Madonna. The redhead succumbs to a dancing frenzy. Slivers of his body licked by the light. Red, green, green, chunks of flesh. A triangle of vest. Half an open mouth. *Hung Up*. A moving shoulder, a thumb. The synth. A hand. The urge to press against that body, see how far it can go. Others are doing it. But it's not the demigod who slides a hand over Oscar's stomach, pulls him back onto a slowly thrusting pelvis. Whoever this is, his face is unimportant. The redhead is gone again. Red-light-green-light-red. The ABBA sample. The hand on his stomach. Madonna's voice... Green-green-red. Whoever's touching him, his face is unimportant. *Hung Up*. The redhead's mouth. The ABBA sample. The whiskey on the breath on his neck. The hand caressing. The pelvis pressing against him. The guts beneath the abs beneath the hand. His breath, whoever this is. The demigod dancing, dancing away. A green elbow. A strip of his face. *Hung Up*. The gin in the guts beneath the hand. His sweating brow. The beer on the guy's breath. Half an afro in the crowd. The girls laughing. Dots in his vision. A glimpse of skin. The synth. The sample. Redhead turns the other way. The whole of his back, red-red-green. Whipping like a cobra. The stranger's hand moving lower. *Hung Up*.

The guy who takes him home might be thirty-eight, might be twenty-two. All that matters is he's led them to a block of flats somewhere off Bethnal Green. And it's about time. Oscar's body is twitching for another.

Did they take the tube? There hovers the memory of a night bus, fragments of a girl in lime green pants trying to pole-dance on the staircase. She had a sort of skin crater on her arm, as if someone mistook her for panacotta and went for it with a spoon. She must've got pretty damn close.

The well-fucked Converse don't fare well against the cold, or the constant friction of the pavement. The guy who leads him along the street is hardy. Nothing more than a T-shirt over his belly, love handles squeezed like toothpaste out of his chinos. The sight of him warms Oscar. Whereas Tim's nose is a delicate slope, this guy's is as pudgy and set as the rest of him. Harmless-looking. When he speaks, vowels stretch and bend like the Mersey from whence he came. *Yew awraaait?*

There's an air of secrecy, even urgency, about the guy. Maybe he's a closet case. Or has a wife.

That worry is laid to rest upon entering his flat. Definite bachelor pad. A room lit as though by candles, made smaller by the box sets of *Battlestar Galactica* and *Game of Thrones*. *Avatar* action figures pose around a twenty-eight-inch monitor while Gambit from *X-Men* spreads his legs over a bookshelf.

The realisation strikes, hard. Oscar's been kidnapped by a geek.

There'd been so many clues, earlier in the evening… Like when the man said he worked close to Forbidden Planet. Should've drunk less, been more awake. They won't have anything in common. This'll be a long night.

'I'm a huge *X-Men* fan,' the guy explains, mistaking Oscar's expression for enthusiasm. Then he waxes geek about his favourite team of superheroes.

And it's not so bad to listen to him talk. His face is so benign, eyes open wide as a child's. And the things he's saying are positive, nice things, about his days as a gay teen yearning for role-model pariahs. *X-Men* fit the bill. Nothing about politics or God or the evils of the moneyed. That's just ego. Socialist babble. This guy is all wonder, and it's pleasant to be around.

His eyes, however, don't so much look into Oscar's as scan his general direction.

In a moment, it clicks. The man is blind. The large monitor, the thick spectacles lying next to it on the desk, the army of half-painted Games Workshop Orcs next to them… The writing was on the wall. A hook-up based on myopia.

But no matter. It's endearing that the guy was insecure enough to go out without his glasses. And he's sighted enough to have found his way to the Underground and back to his place.

After all these months, perhaps it's better if Oscar's body is only glimpsed in the dark, out of focus.

'Do you like Joss Whedon?' the guy asks.

'Is she related to Joss Stone?'

The guy blinks. 'Joss Whedon is a man,' he says, laughing.

And relatives share surnames, not first names. But it's OK. There's no mockery in the man's laugh. He thinks Oscar's being cute. 'Joss Whedon is the guy who wrote *Buffy*?'

'Oh, yeah. The vampire.'

'Vampire slayer, yeah. And he did this awesome series called *Firefly*, which was about... well, "space cowboys", for want of a better expression. Makes it sound dumb but it really isn't.'

'No, it sounds fun.'

'Yeah, it's really funny actually! But it was cancelled by the network after twelve episodes.'

'Oh, how sad.'

The man blinks. 'Well, it's kind of a cult classic now so all is not lost.'

He's the sort of man-boy that women love to mother. Cuddly, shy smile, facial gymnastics of a cartoon. It makes Oscar wonder how he looks to others, in conversation or deep in thought. What manoeuvres his features perform while he's unconscious of them. Or when he's self-conscious, out on a balcony with a cigarette in his hand.

Bella's eyes narrow when she talks of personal matters, shrink to emerald points in the black mascara. But when she's launching a tirade — on Christians, Tories, Meninists, Fascists, Lukas — her eyes explode with disbelief. Her tongue pokes out every now and then to moisten her lips. Proof that she, too, is mortal. That her opinions dry her out as well.

Charlotte laughs with her lips sealed. Sometimes her hand shoots up to cover her mouth, to keep the giggles from escaping too unladylike. Face and voice of a fairy godmother, but when she's concentrating, lost in her work, she looks hell-bent on killing. Even though she's writing bollocks.

Terry hardly ever made eye contact. It was only to say, *I want you. Right this second.* They must've spent a year of their relationship avoiding each other's gaze. Blushing. Anytime their eyes met, and stayed there, it was like a really shit perfume advert. The faces Terry made during sex, stolen from black-and-white TV commercials where chicks in Nina Ricci roll around in limos over the Seine, fitting with ecstasy. It must've been like that the first time with him, on that single bed. But there's only tenderness in the memory. A soft kiss, a deep longing. The simple need to press warm skin against warm skin, to be enveloped by someone's love. *It's OK,* Terry said. *I love you.* And Oscar believed it.

Tim would be different. He might not even look at him, might not even say he loved him. He'd just be certain he was pleasing him right. Or, even better, he might look right into him. Communicate without words.

The pleasant geek's been admiring him. He's another one who avoids eye contact until his head is filled with sex. And the time has come to put aside all shame.

He walks over to a bedside table, bends to open a drawer. He takes out lube and a pack of condoms.

'No names,' he says, cheeks red.

Oscar's mouth is parched, filled with something rotten. His heart rattles.

'I'm sorry if that seems cold. But I was with my ex for five years, and I'm still ... kind of getting over it.'

Jeans and boxer shorts drying on the radiator.

The damp heat clogs his nostrils, makes him breathe through his mouth. The Eye is at his chest.

The guy steps forward. Takes Oscar by the hands, as if they're standing at the altar. It's nothing but a union, a physical union.

The guy lunges at him. Presses his lips to Oscar's, hot mouth over his, tongue swirling around. There's the trace of Sambuca on it, untouched by the breath mint. 'Mmm,' he says. 'You taste sweet.'

It's when the guy turns his back and pulls down his own chinos, the blue Aussiebum boxer-briefs, that it dawns on Oscar what's expected of him. And it's something he can't deliver. It doesn't work this way. No-one's ever thought this of him. His heart is pounding. The only thing in his head is a word he can't remember, the blank space it leaves behind — a part of the brain that is either bigger or smaller when a person is gay, a thing beginning with H.

'Just… get these off,' the guy says in a mumsy voice, Charlotte's voice, as he pulls down his boxer-briefs. At the sight of the round white buttocks, Oscar's eyes shoot up to the back of the guy's head. That's another thing that says someone's gay. The hair goes anticlockwise from the crown. Or is it clockwise? His leg is trembling.

The guy tears the foil, takes out a condom, passes it back to Oscar. The smell of the latex jolts him awake.

'Sorry. Sorry.'

It falls from his hands to the floor. The guy stays bent over his desk, Games Workshop orcs felled by his movements. His head sinks into the crook of his arm, and he won't turn to face the terrified boy behind him.

'Sorry. Sorry.'

The guy's sobs follow Oscar out into the corridor, down the stairs, where he's soon swallowed up by the darkness.

Lukas' flat is stuffy from his weed smoke, so Bella interrupts the game to open a window. It's only gone seven but the night is a deep black. They race for another minute before Lukas makes the finish line, winner, while Bella hobbles along in eighth place.

'Aw, bad luck, B,' says Maya, before complaining that she's hungry and that Lukas should feed his guests. 'Who's up for Thai?'

Lukas whips out his laptop and types. 'Nepalese is better.' He mentions a place with Yak in the name, which he claims is the best takeaway South of the river.

'Lukas,' Bella says, 'if there is actual yak in this food I'm going to stab you with this Wii controller.'

It's a thought that haunts Oscar. It's in his head when the food arrives, the spicy warmth of it sweeping the flat like a wave as Maya carries it in. His curry sits on its bed of rice with all the possibility of being yak. *What's the difference?* Terry would've said, like the time they saw that sign in the shop window, *BONELESS CAMEL MEAT SOLD HERE*. The thought of a camel's hump being chomped by a human jaw, of its flesh being ripped from its bones… Sent a shudder up Oscar's spine, no matter how many times Terry said he seemed perfectly happy to eat cow.

'Go on, B,' Maya says, 'give it here.' She takes the controller, changes the driver and vehicle. The characters and menus and courses flash before them, bright, loud, Japanese, and Maya screams as Lukas overtakes her. She pummels him, on-screen and off, until she takes the lead. Rather than watching the action, Bella watches the players. Then she looks at the floor as if someone has died.

She only stirs again when Lukas mentions Terry. 'He messaged me earlier,' he says, grabbing a handful of peanuts from a bowl on the table. 'He was asking if we could hang out when he comes.'

Oscar's head has turned despite him, while Maya keeps hers tellingly straight.

'What an arse,' Bella says. 'What did you tell him?'

'Nothing, I just… led him to believe I lived with you guys.' He smiles. 'I didn't want to be rude, innit.'

'You should be fucking rude, he's a knob.' She made an enemy of Terry when he broke up with Oscar, got herself a Twitter account when he unfriended her on Facebook. An Instagram one when she was blocked on Twitter.

Maya moves her legs on the sofa, the plastic cover squeaking beneath her. At another time, she would tell Bella to be reasonable, that Terry is simply lost and trying to find himself. It's none of their business what he did, and not their place to judge. But Oscar's in the room now, so she keeps her words locked up. She's so decent it's hurtful.

'Look, man, I wasn't friendly. I wasn't rude but I wasn't friendly. I just said I might see him at Mal's party, 'cause he was talking about going.'

'Did you tell him we'd be there?'

'Yeah.'

Bella nods. 'OK. If he knows Osky and I are going, maybe he won't come.'

Naan in hand, Maya carries on flicking through the character options on screen without uttering a word. It takes no time for Lukas to rejoin her. Bella watches the screen, dead-eyed.

Now the curry isn't even yak anymore. It's camel, and Oscar can't bring himself to eat it.

Tim hasn't replied to his text.

He'd better stop listening to the mixtape, or it'll drive him to distraction. It isn't some sort of Enigma code for him to work through. It's not a confession, not a coming-out ceremony through tape. Only a man's taste in music shared with a friend. At best, Oscar is a project to him, a thing young enough to be moulded. And Tim is a reverse Jehovah's Witness, with a different god.

He likes having someone to affect, stokes his ego.

Or Oscar is a way of killing time.

In Oscar's head, he and Tim have been together for years. They have a flat in Covent Garden, Julianne Moore drops in to say hi, he and Tim push and punch each other playfully, tell each other to fuck off (but laugh about it). Host dinner parties for friends. Tim's urbane, uni-educated friends who have degrees in Classics and Politics. One of them the half-Thai/half-whatever ex-girlfriend who's happy to see Tim happy.

He and Tim in bed. Waking up together, falling asleep together. The spirals of hair on the man's crown, flowing the right way. This other person's head next to his. The two of them breathing together, talking in constellations.

On the sofa. On the tube. Walking through a crowd. Chinatown. Chinese New Year, like that time with Charlotte, when they hit Gerrard Street and found themselves trapped in a sea of people, thick as tar. So tightly packed there was no point in walking at all. The bodies could have carried them, feet in the air, to the other end. The slowest crowdsurf in history.

The mixtape rolls on. A song called *Habit* starts to play, and he and Tim are breaking up. It's tearful, for both of them, and there's the warm damp smell of shorts drying on a radiator as Tim announces he's leaving. He doesn't want Oscar, never really did.

It's this woman's voice that brings a lump to his throat. The pitch of it.

For one more minute,

Let our habit become small.

One more minute of Tim. That's all.

Then Tim grows older on his own. Making stir-fry, listening to Captain Beefheart, singing along. And once in a while he recalls that boy who used to stand in corners watching him, waiting for nothing, and be glad to be shot of that. He's capable of it. If everyone's just bodies, then they're just bodies. Whether sex or amputation, a limb is a limb is a limb. To Tim, Oscar is a scrap of veal. A boy with a head somewhat too large for his frame, like all boys, and ginger to boot. A waist the size of a wrist. Delicate, yes, pretty, yes, with hazel eyes and feminine lips. But nothing to turn your head. Nothing to feel the lack of.

Tim is only blood, and nerves, and meat. He isn't Oscar's to demand or crave. You're not his and he's not yours. Stop thinking about him calling, or apologising for not calling. He will never say, *I've loved you since the moment you—* even though you don't know when he could have fallen for you. He couldn't have. He's incapable. He lacks that function, that gene. Whatever you're looking for, it's not with him. Wash your head. Get him out of it. Don't give a shit.

Tim is such a small part of his life anyway, a mere fraction. He never even knew the man existed until a couple of months ago. This whole city existed before them both. The Thames even longer, same goes for bridges, banks and benches. Even some of the people walking about, tourists and OAPs admiring the sights, existed in different countries and continents long before either he or Tim was born. The river, the sea, volcanoes spewing ash clouds and tsunamis that engulf cities. The patch of earth called Lunduntown. They've all been around for millennia. Even bits of his DNA, whatever he's sprung from — chimp or duchess, bookie or Zumba instructor — was passed down from descendant to descendant to descendant, and it'll end with him. The last link.

Tim is human. Many components that together formed a stimulant. A stimulant for an eager boy to react to. He's a body that began as blood, grew into a man, developed his tastes and beliefs through neither his nor God's choice, and happened to come to the patch of earth that eventually turned into London. That's it.

Charlotte's book group natters away on the other side of the wall, Belgravia's voice clear above all the other ladies'. She's started going quiet on Oscar's entrances, changing the subject. Once they've gone, Charlotte tiptoes into Oscar's room without knocking, puts a cup of tea down on his bedside table and gently squeezes his thigh. 'My sweet little boy...'

She's heard from Tim. No doubt about it. He texts her every day.

She lingers, sits on her son's bed next to him, the air between them packed. But she only sighs, knowing that anything she said would be wrong.

She must never know about Oscar's feelings. It would only make her feel a bad mother.

09 COMMUNION

Sunny days have been dropping to frosty nights. But before anyone can get cosy in a thick-knit jumper, it's back to being warm and sunny. There's no way there'll be snow this year, not like that winter a few years back when the city almost sank in it. That thick white layer changed the place. Altered familiar sights, turned outdoor stations into Moscow. People huddled on platforms, waiting for delayed trains and cursing the cancelled services. *For fuck's sake* every time a suicide was announced through the tannoy.

The horoscope readings on the app are equally unclear. One day the outlook's bright, the next it seems nothing is aligned. Patience will come to bear.

And out of the blue, in the midst of a reading, Oscar's phone buzzes with a text. The Olympics have never seen such lightning moves.

It's from Tim. The horoscope was right— there has been contact from a special someone.

Saw an old lady in the park speaking Creole to nobody visible and thought of you. T.

There is no clear way to respond. Nothing in Oscar's personal history has prepared him for this scenario. He should raid Charlotte's bookshelves, find a self-help tome that might provide the answers. *What to Do When Your Man Compares You to a Caribbean Nutjob*. It all comes back to his childhood, basic etiquette. *What Would Charlotte Do?*

LOL is too simple. *OMG* feeble. And neither of them is the right mix —of elegance, wit, sex appeal— that his reply needs to be. It'll take some thought. Rushing to reply would look desperate. After weeks of drought, weeks of hope, another minute can't hurt.

The sky in his bedroom window is grey. The sills, the mantlepiece, the duvet are cold to the touch. Rain has always been a hopeful sign for him. All is being wiped clean, refreshed. The pavements and cars and post-boxes, bins, parking metres, everything. People have been walking around in T-shirts with their shades on for weeks. Things have been glinting, practically blinding. About time for a change. But people feel cheated and moan, curse the British weather. Even the weather has a nationality.

The fact is, Tim witnessed a happening out of the ordinary and thought of him. First. Didn't need to say anything, didn't need to text, but he did. It's not a story he can share with others, least of all Charlotte, because it wouldn't make the same impression. No matter how much time Oscar and Bella spend together, they will always be wired differently. They look the same species, sound the same, but one speaks a language and the other speaks its dialect. She can knock him down with a pretty observation, yet refuse to see the beauty that stuns him. When they ended up at Lukas' flat one night and put on a film they'd never heard of, Bella spent most of it yelling at the screen to fuck off. Affronted by the film's warped structure, its leaps in logic, its senseless characters, she hated it all. Meanwhile, Oscar struggled to fight back tears. Every frame spoke to him, every moment hurt. But he couldn't admit that. Not while Bella was flicking peanuts at the screen.

Whatever his response to the text, it must only be understood by him and Tim. The man might even smile as he reads it.

God responds to all dialects. O.

He'll like that. It's a good day.

It's Mal's party but she's nowhere to be seen. Not that she and Oscar ever hang out, but it's faintly troubling when the hostess is absent from her shindig. They've turned up the heat in this place to compensate for the weather outside. But while you could sauté mushrooms on Oscar's face, his feet take their time to thaw. Starlings of light fly around the ceiling, pass over plastic chandeliers before shooting down into the chattering bodies and out of sight.

Maya fucked off with a guy called Louis half an hour ago, and now Oscar's trapped between a pleather sofa and some chick who sees orbs. She sits close, swishes her rum-and-Coke past his face to point to a corner of the room. 'There,' she says. 'Three of them. One that's a bit bigger than the other two and sort of at head level?'

It's like the ghost-hunting shows on TV, people screaming in Nightvision cellars.

She laughs. 'You're looking with your brain,' she says. 'Not with your soul.'

Bella swoops in, holding drinks. 'Oh Oscar, don't tell me you're not looking with your soul *again*.' She puts a fresh G&T in his hand. 'I tell you, it's his biggest flaw.'

The girl giggles.

'So who are you today?' Bella says.

'What do you mean?'

'Weren't you an Egyptian priestess last time we met?'

The girl smiles. 'That's not how it works. Another incarnation of me was a priestess. In a past life. Remember, I was telling you about regression—'

'Right. So with this past-life stuff,' Bella interrupts, pointing with her own G&T, 'there's something I don't understand. I mean, how come you're only experiencing Now?'

The girl creases her eyebrows, leans in. 'I don't follow.'

'If you're a hundred different people in there, how come you're only experiencing You as You Right Now, the way I see you?'

'Because it's now.'

'So you have no memory of hanging with Tutankhamun?'

'You mean, like, memories from my past lives?'

'Yeah.'

'I can access them. You just need to see with different eyes.' She checks Oscar's face to see if this registers.

'So it's almost as though they're a completely different person whose life you imagine.'

'No, she's me. They're all me.'

'Who are the others?'

'Well, one of them was a duchess in Victorian England—'

'What year?'

'Uh… I dunno— 1860?'

'Shit. Go on.'

'… And one of them is from Kolkata.'

'Do you speak Bengali?'

'No, but I'd love to learn.'

'Why don't you know it?'

'What?' The girl giggles. 'I'm well confused!'

'Me too. I mean, how come you don't know her language, since you are her?'

'But right now I'm me. At this point in time.'

'But isn't language a memory? Isn't it, in fact, a long-term memory? Can't you access that?'

The girl thinks about this. 'Language is more to do with the brain, though. I'm talking about the soul.'

'What is the soul?'

The girl laughs. 'Uh… feelings? Talent?'

'So do you share their talents? Like, was the duchess a wiz with a loom?'

'No!' the girl laughs. 'That's so random.'

Bella laughs too. 'We all are. So what talents do you share?'

'Um… I suppose my singing voice, I get that from the priestess.'

'I see. So what happened to all the prozzies?'

'Sorry?'

'The slappers, the wenches on the docks. Didn't they have souls? Why do prostitutes never do a *Being John Malkovich* and get in someone else's body too? Or cleaners, what about cleaners? Or, like, balding accountants from the seventies?'

The girl's eyes narrow as she cottons on. 'I'm sure they do,' she says. 'They're just not me.' Then she turns to spot someone she knows across the room. Gets up, straightens her dress. 'Excuse me,' she says to the air, and leaves.

Bella meets Oscar's eye and exhales.

It makes him feel awful, the way Bella stoned the girl. Recalls Charlotte going red at Claridge's on their anniversary. The queasiness it brings with it.

'Sorry I didn't save you sooner, Oskovich. I was late on account of Lukas being a vain knob.'

She takes a big gulp, rests the empty glass on the bay windowsill. A spot covered in flyers of gigs and discounted drinks.

She and Lukas came together. Got ready together. But she doesn't elaborate, only scrolls through Facebook on her phone as she sips her G&T.

He can't tell her about the text from Tim, or the times he's visited since. The new smile on the man's face when he greets him now, that code between them, the handshakes and shoulder-pats bordering on Masonic. They've talked about the tracks on the mixtape, Tim delighted at his good choice of gift. The man's leaned in to look at Oscar's head, where the bruises have faded to a jaundiced cloud. It's beginning to feel more and more like they've already had sex, in Charlotte's bed while she was scribbling notes in her Moleskine journals. She'll glance up once in a while, to entertain the fantasy of her fake son and youthful boyfriend getting along. The way she planned it. But of course, one can only dream. The sin of it, the out-and-out crime.

It'll happen. Their time will come.

The only person to confide these impure thoughts to is Maya. She'd listen with a cup of Rooibos warming her hands, and tell him to look within himself. Seeing her features crumple at a friend's distress would be enough to make him stronger.

'Oh my God,' says Bella, turning her phone to him. 'Guess where Mal is. She's in the toilets having a panic attack, all over Twitter. Nice of her to take the time to inform us, the twat.' She takes out her phone and scrolls down. 'Holy shit, she's updated again. We're in the same building!' She glances over towards the toilets, where a crowd has gathered. Laughing, she turns back to her phone and points out all the grammatical errors in Mal's updates.

'Don't…' But his voice is too quiet, can't be heard above the noise.

'Do you think I should reply with a motivational quote against a sunset?'

Bella's going to be hated one day, if she isn't already. The invites will stop coming, and she'll sit alone in her room, full of loathing for everybody. So much so it'll keep her from reading. It's as if that's what she wants. Sammy once told them about a type of gun, hell-dangerous for firing bullets in all directions. *Shoot and Pray*, they call it. You get near that puppy, say your prayers. That's Bella through and through, and people will learn to scatter. Whereas Mal will always be loved. Never mind that a hundred years ago she'd've been dumped in Bedlam, chained to a wall. Or that, actually, she is a twat.

Bella's arm darts out to save him, as if Oscar was about to fall. She's going to share another update from Mal, something even more outrageous. But no, the look on her face says otherwise. Her eyes are fixed on a boy across the room, who's come upon Lukas and is leaning in for an awkward hug.

Terry.

In England. In this room.

Bella doesn't speak. Oscar couldn't if he wanted to. It's as if by keeping quiet, they'll somehow evade his detection. But it doesn't take long for the boy to turn in their direction. He sees them, no more than a second, before turning away again.

Bella swears under her breath. Lukas keeps up the chit-chat, but his friendliness, usually offered to anyone and everyone, is kept on a tight lead. He doesn't speak much, and looks over at Oscar and Bella whenever Terry is distracted. A few others have gathered 'round, ready with hugs and kisses for the boy from Tokyo, who's changed, who's a different person now, dead and unfeeling and just plain rude, who is childishly not turning 'round to look again, or come over to say something, who isn't even a patch on a more important man, not by a long shot.

Before he's even aware of it, Oscar's off his seat. Bella tries to call him back, but she's far behind him now. The other bodies pass by in his vision like buildings in a car window, one of them Terry's, left behind with the closing of the bar door.

Sometime around two, they ended up at Lukas' place. Maya resurfaced, held Oscar's hand all the way on the night bus to Clapham. Not ten minutes after they entered the flat, Lukas stripped to his boxers to go to bed. Maya tried to deter him, so they could all stay up together for a bit. Hugged him and jumped onto his back, sang into his ear, put a Wii controller in his hands. But it took a handful of peanuts and a couple of tokes on a joint to wake him up, after which he soon got drowsy again. Bella was downcast throughout, until she turned her back on the sofa and fell asleep before everyone else. By five, Oscar was still awake. The small green light of Lukas' laptop charging on the table, shining on bowls and bongs, kept him from sleep.

Now he's out in the streets of Clapham, his shoes too feeble for the walk home. The air soaks them, freezing his feet. Seemed like a good idea at the time, to leave. But where can he go to? Only Charlotte's, back home to Mummy. Churns his stomach, but the thought appeals all the same. He should've stayed in the warmth of Lukas' flat, spooning Bella. Halfwit. He shouldn't have left her. She was in a mood, and nobody else could tell. Or at least they pretended not to. He should've been there for her, 'til she started laughing at other people's grammar once more.

There's a tube-map app on his phone, but that won't be any use. He's nowhere near the Clapham tube stops and there's no WiFi to figure out how to get to them, or data left over. The thought of walking to one in this wintry night, in this flimsy jacket (what a nincompoop. Layers, they tell you), is a joke. The only hope is to catch another night bus, or hop on an overground train to within the vicinity of Charlotte's, then walk from there if he can guess the way.

He's screwed.

The terraced houses sit quiet, dark, hiding imminent death around each corner. Knife-wielding teens. Blind cars. Terry. But there's nothing, which is even worse.

If only he knew where Tim lived. It won't be West London, that much is clear.

Tim's smile was so big, so genuinely full, the last time he saw Oscar. Eyed him up and down as though they might never meet again. Then he remembered himself and tried to downplay it. That stubbled jaw, that almost-red hair. If only he were here now, if he appeared in the distance. He'll transpire in the middle of this maze and guide him to the train.

What a wanker. What a stupid thing to think. As if he's been lost in the desert for days, parched and seeing mirages. Nothing's going to happen, because Tim is in bed somewhere, maybe even with Charlotte, and Oscar's just a scrap of a thing walking down a street, one of the million streets of London's suburbs.

A hooded figure steps into the road.

This is it. The end.

Stabbed to death in Clapham, found slumped over a speed bump, wearing the wrong shoes for walking. But the man hasn't even noticed him, would probably shit a brick if he did, and carries on about his business. There's a sign pointing to the station. Thank God. If there are any trains, that is. The probability of a night bus grows.

Terry wouldn't even speak to him tonight, the cunt. All those weeks of stress, arguments running through his head in the shower. Or while peeing, all those nightmare imaginings of how their reunion would play out. In some of these, Oscar was strong, possessed of a RuPaul fierceness. Spilled his drink on the rat, strutted off in stilettos. In other visions he was charming, verged on aloof. Terry was sorry.

He should've guessed how this would go. This is exactly how Terry portrayed himself whenever he spoke of his exes.

Something moves, a few feet away. A fox crawls out from under a car, stops in the middle of the road. It meets his gaze, holds it, and they both stay frozen for a long minute. The creature is thinner in the face than he ought to be, less bushy in the tail. They say not to look in an animal's eyes, that for them it's a confrontation. But there's only curiosity here. A bit of fear, on both sides. The fox breaks the spell, flicks his eyes away first and trots along down the street.

It's the closest a fox has ever been to him, an event worth celebrating. What the hell, make it a holiday. His birthday. The something of November, or December, the day a fox looked him right in the eye. Something else should happen, like he should turn into gold, or his hands fall off, for the sake of mythology. What would it make him, to be born in November? Virgo. Sagittarius. Maya says he must be a Pisces. Everyone says he must be a Pisces, whatever that means.

No matter. At least it won't be a general reading on the horoscope app from now on. Virgo sounds good. Or Sagittarius. Centaur with a crossbow.

Stranger things have happened.

Tim invites them both to dinner. Charlotte accepts, nothing in her attitude suggesting Oscar would be a third wheel. Maybe there's nothing to this after all, no matter what the rags in the newsagents say. The pictures of Charlotte and Tim, *TOY BOY*. Even those basic office bitches clicking away on Photoshop thinking him hot.

The evening comes. As they wait for Charlotte to powder her nose, Tim leads the way to the balcony. He salutes Carolina as he passes, in a manner that befits a captain. And she laughs, playfully bats him with a towel. As far as Oscar's aware, she's never even smiled before in her entire life. She grew up in a country with no Mickey Mouse.

Outside, Tim in a white shirt and a pumpkin jumper, the man hears all about Terry's behaviour at the bar, nods along gravely. 'Knob'ead,' he says, which makes Oscar laugh. 'He should've at least acknowledged you.'

'Yeah, well…' It seemed a better tactic to downplay the effect of Terry's actions, to appear cool and above the whole business. But now it might've backfired. Tim might think him casual about life in general. A happy slut who once fell under a youth called Terry or Teri or Tehrí amongst a dozen others.

'When did you two break up?'

It's not reconnaissance, only interest. 'Ju— uh, June.'

'Wow. That's quite a while. Have you… seen anyone since?'

'Nah, it's…'

But the sentence hangs there.

Tim looks him dead-on as he brings the cigarillo to his mouth. 'It'll happen when it happens,' he says. 'If you even want it to happen, that is.'

Now. Now is the time to say it. 'Yeah… Lately, there's been— Like, I've been thinking about it.'

Tim smiles, but something flickers in his eye. Something like a warning, a signal to drop the subject.

Charlotte's heels come clicking along on the other side of the French windows. 'Ready, boys!'

Tim stubs his smoke out. 'You heard the woman!'

'Tim—' And his hand is on the man's arm, a shock to them both. Static from the jumper buzzes on his fingers. 'Sorry. Don't tell Charlotte, please? About Terry?'

'Oh, yeah. OK.'

'It'll upset her.'

Her lover smiles. 'You're right,' he says, 'it would.'

It's hard to divine what he meant by that. Whether Charlotte has already spoken with him about it. And if she has, what did she say? How did she paint the ordeal? Needy, pathetic Oscar. First-world problems without an end in sight.

The subject bothers him all through the tube ride, Charlotte and Tim finding two free spaces across from an empty single with his name on it, sandwiched between a lady reading the Bible and someone's Planet Organic horde. It's only black people who read the Bible, judging by London transport. Makes him afraid to be a sodomite. But this woman's nice-looking. All smart shoes and hot lips, a calm demeanour. She'd be a good Christian, loving her neighbour and feeding orphans. Like Charlotte.

Next stop is Hammersmith. Tim leads them out into the streets, Charlotte's eyes flicking around in search of youths, and into a Lebanese restaurant by the flyover. Inside it's warm, the scent of food heavenly. Herbs and spices, lamb and feta. Tim takes Charlotte through the menu, pointing out the meze he thinks she'd like and she, like a Barbie, saying things like, 'You order for us! I trust your judgment.' The bimbo. Ditz. And the way they look at each other when the waitress skedaddles with their order, grinning, kids in school, is a clear step beyond friendship. *TOY BOY. Hot young lover for golden-girl author.* When Oscar's eyes fall to the table, there's the sound of a quick peck on the lips. Then the parting of their faces, leaving what definitely happened only in his head.

The food takes little time to come. Hummus scooped up with pitta, a sprinkling of pine nuts adding extra bite. Batata harra and kibbeh, tabbouleh and minced lamb in deep-fried pastry.

Charlotte pronounces the food delicious, practically fucking knights it, and makes them all clink their glasses in cheers to Tim's good taste.

'I'm gonna sound so English, though,' the man says, 'and ask for a brew. D'you think they'll throw us out?'

They don't. The cute brown-eyed waitress laughs at his order, probably used to customers needing a bit of Brit with the ethnic by now, and within minutes brings a 'brew' over to the table. Such an attractive thing to call a cup of tea, so much more interesting. A story in itself — *brew*.

Charlotte finds it funny, pats his arm as she brings a glass of red to her mouth. Then she stops. She's spotted something behind her almost-son. 'Oh Oscar, look!'

Hanging by his head on the wall is a larger version of the Eye, the glimmer of tea-lights along its surface.

After dinner Tim takes them to a pub. It's a Victorian gal made of neat brickwork, bay windows of curved glass. Borders, sills and ledges painted purple, the door an olive green. Inside there's a chandelier, and countless other lamps of differing shapes and sizes, some with fabric shades, some glass, hanging over the spacious bar. Groups of people sit on stools around high tables, ensconced in the booths. So much merriment, so much noise.

As Tim and Charlotte venture ahead in search of an empty space, a mild panic seizes Oscar. The other two sprint for a sofa vacated by a bigger group. And by Charlotte's reaction, it's hilariously lower than it looks. She's being obvious. Showing everyone what a united family they are, what a whale of a time they're having.

'You should've been here when Kate Bush was on around the corner,' Tim says. 'They played her songs on a loop.'

'Oh God,' says Charlotte with a grimace. 'The poor staff!'

Of course she hates the Bush. Of course she does. And she and Tim quibble about that adorably. For a while, Oscar's attention is hooked by the clocks that hang in a row above the doorway. The middle one goes anticlockwise, the numbers reversed on its face. Makes his eyes sting.

Then it happens. Tim goes off to fetch the drinks, leaving Oscar alone with Charlotte. He must think they'd be fine together, a mother and son with a history of warmth and love between them. But the seconds pass, filled with the loudness of others around them, people in good company.

Eventually, Charlotte puts her hand on his knee. 'Are you alright, my darling?' And she smiles, patiently, as though she knows he's tired.

Then, some relief. A fan of Charlotte's has spotted her. It's usually annoying when a stranger interrupts them, but tonight a fangirl's intrusion is welcome. Woman clocked Charlotte from a mile off, maybe even from outside, through a telescope, such is her glee.

'I've literally, literally, just finished your book. Hang on.' And she rifles through her bag, digs out the victim of her fervour. Girl must be a riot in the sack.

'Would you like me to sign it for you?' Charlotte says.

'OhmyGodwouldyou?'

The author laughs. 'Of course!'

But the woman doesn't have a pen. She's so embarrassed, she always has a pen usually, like, literally always on her. So Charlotte gets out her fountain pen, because it adds meaning to her signature, and the woman goes off a grateful mess.

Then, like a girlfriend, Charlotte turns to Oscar. 'Quick,' she says, 'before he comes back. What do you think of Tim?'

At last, she's said it. And it stumps him. After all that excitement, a chance for the truth to come between them. Enough bullshit.

I like him.

But now is not the time. Tim is twisting his body to weave between the others, three glasses pressed together in his hands.

'Yeah, he's nice.'

Which was the right thing to say, because the happiness in Charlotte's face is the same as when she thought he loved the Macbook. And it shines even brighter once Tim has set the drinks down on the table, and reclaimed his seat, again lower than expected, beside her. When she's sitting in a pub, carefree, with her two favourite men. A family.

Charlotte insists on a cab home, claiming she feels too unsteady to take the tube again. And for a few minutes on the ride back to Kensington, the lovers crack. The subject of Maggie Thatcher has come up, via Pistorius, South African gun crime and Nelson Mandela. And it's the first time, maybe because of the drink, that Charlotte speaks in harsh tones to Tim. 'Don't be cruel,' she says. 'The woman did not deserve to have people laugh at her death.'

'She didn't give a shit about the people whose lives she destroyed,' Tim answers back, 'so why should I? Especially when she's dead, and can't even hear what I'm saying.'

'It's disrespectful.'

'First of all, she's dead. And second … she doesn't deserve respect.'

'Everybody does.'

'No, everybody must earn it. Nobody should have it automatically. Otherwise we'd respect Putin and Pinochet and even bloody Oscar Pistorius. Remember Belgrano?'

'It's cruel to laugh at an old lady's death.'

'OK, then tell me this …' And his voice, to Oscar's surprise, starts to quiver. 'Why were people so happy to see her die? Her specifically, no other British politician. It's not just a case of left wing and right wing, otherwise we'd party every time a Tory kicked the bucket. You must admit that for people to react that way, she must've had a huge negative effect. It went beyond disagreeing with her policies. The eighties were a flippin' civil *war*, and another one's coming. Her legacy is a ruined country.'

In the slivers of street-light that pass over her face, Charlotte's expression is ice-cold. But then she takes a sudden turn. 'Oscar darling, what do you think?'

In the window of the cab, a shabby-looking man is heaving by a lamppost. It's hard to even swallow, what with Tim and Charlotte heating up, let alone form an opinion. Tim does his best not to move around on the opposite seat as the cab takes a corner. His eyes are fixed on the boy, amber in the flickering light. 'Remember Clause Twenty-eight,' he says, which means nothing to Oscar.

'Shh!'

Tim's argument was compelling, damn near emotional, but Charlotte does have a point. The part of him that wanted to please Tim is quiet, almost noiseless. 'Someone's mother got old and died.'

Tim rolls his eyes and hangs his head, theatrically.

'Spoken like a good little boy!' says Charlotte, and hugs Oscar to her.

Tim sighs. 'OK, fine. Two against one. But she was still a hateful bitch and I'm glad she's dead.'

The words are a shock to Oscar's system. Bone-rattling. Make him wonder if he'd feel that strongly had he grown up under Thatcher's hand. It never occurred to him before that Tim and Bella are essentially the same — the zeal that lights them both up, makes him a moth to a flame. And it's suddenly not he or Charlotte who should be with the man, but the girl who eyeballs Witnesses, who enjoys the sight of an ailing prick in a jar. Who's a Liberal amongst Conservatives.

No. It's not a romance Bella needs, 'cause what would she do with it? She's never even made it clear if she's lost her virginity. No-one's brought it up, from fear of causing offence. Her flirtations after Terry left were more funny than suggestive, and her physical discomfort speaks volumes. She can't go ten seconds without adjusting her T-shirt, seems calmer in winter layers. Even then she tugs at jumpers, covers her arms, folds her hands over her stomach when there's nothing else to occupy her hands. A girl so awkward with her body can't be sexual enough to share it. With an old Norwegian maybe, but not with Tim.

Somewhere out there, there are photos of the 'ugly' younger Bella, the one she refers to every so often as if she's in the next room. *The lard-arse of Christmas past*, the girl who inhaled turkeys between meals. Her fat body slimmed to the girth of chicken wire, but she doesn't seem to know it. Might be stretch marks under her arms, or a deep-rooted longing for Battenberg she wrestles on a daily basis. But her old self has melted away. Instead of confidence it left behind a raw creature, all nerves, which she's turned paranoid trying to protect. Her talk of *wanting to be nice* to guys is all show. Misdirection. All she wants is a job.

In no time at all, the cab pulls up outside the block. As they stumble out of it, it seems the tension between Charlotte and Tim has blown away. Or transformed, become a different energy. They look at each other, bleary, hold hands as they go upstairs.

From the other side of the French windows, as the smoke pours out through his nose and mouth, the lovers call good-night to Oscar, left alone outside on the balcony. The smooth click of the bedroom door as it shuts behind them.

They'll be kissing. Tim unbuttoning his shirt. That taut body underneath. And Charlotte, pressing him close to her. Lowering his shorts. Pulling him into the bed. He'll remember she liked Thatcher and he won't go easy on her.

Oscar doesn't even have a job.

Clapham Junction. It was the right decision. Despite his speed, people push past him. Ozzies screech about a chick named Tonya. A bunch of thirty-year-olds dressed like school-boys, short sleeves in the night chill, still no bastard snow, hands deep in their pockets. The tiles along the walls shoot past him, single colours at random on the white. Red, blue, grey, blue-grey, red-grey, blue, red-blue, grey. A siren's howling, flying through the tunnel of the walkway, down the stairs of the platform exits, a robot-woman's voice on loop. Will *Inspector Sands... please contact Control? Will Inspector Sands... please contact Control? Will Inspector Sands... please contact Control?* She keeps going, woman possessed, and everybody looks around amused, at each other, puzzled, covering their ears. Nobody's panicked. This might be code. For terrorists, bombs, ISIS. Seventh of July in December. It's happening, the new London Blitz. Fire, youths and guns. It spurs him on. Sends him through the barriers, slamming his Oyster card on the reader, making a beeline for Lavender Hill.

The night is clear, the traffic signals are clear, the drunken whoops and chants, the empty Jägermeister rolling on the pavement, the winding route all the way to Lukas' flat. Reasonable hours can go to Hell.

After the pounding of his fists on the door, a stillness.

After that, a muffled clink, followed by the soft shuffle of naked feet on carpet on wood. The door opens, a punch of pot. Lukas sees him, does a double-take. 'Were we going out?'

'Is Terry here?'

Lukas looks stunned. 'What the fuck? No, man. What's up?' He shows Oscar in, invites him to sit on the plastic-covered sofa. It only works if you wipe the plastic from time to time, dude. The control pad of the Nintendo Wii-U rests on the glass-topped table by a bong and a bowl of peanuts. 'Something up?' he says, not joining Oscar on the sofa. 'You don't look too good.'

And with that, Oscar's nerve is shot. There's no reason to be here, nothing to achieve. From his position on the sofa, everything seems bigger and more important than him. The posters on the wall, Lukas' afro, the bump in his boxers.

Lukas sits down next to him, the plastic cover making a noise. 'Dude... You need to tell someone.' His gentle hand on Oscar's back is like a slap.

Before Oscar can ask how he knows, a soft voice behind him. 'Osky...?' At the door, in a large T-shirt and sweatpants, is Bella.

10 GONE LIKE YESTERDAY

He's woken up by a dog barking, and pigeons fighting over a bag of chips. It takes a while for it to sink in where he is, what's happened. Where his mattress went, why his bed is a wooden bench. And why the dresser and wardrobe and fireplace in his bedroom look like trees and dogs and housewives doing tai chi en masse. Asleep in the park like a tramp. Lucky not to have been stabbed, or robbed. Press-ganged into some South London criminal network. People must've thought him homeless, a junkie. He sure as hell must look like one.

People are staring. Time to wander off, as if it had only been a ten-minute power-nap before work.

On the green, a man throws a squeaky toy at his yelping, happy mongrel. Every time the dog returns, tail wagging, mouth squeaking like a mad thing, his owner rubs his head and ponders the beast with a big goofy grin. Then he yanks the toy, wet with slobber, out of the dog's mouth and hurls it into the distance. The dog's already darted in the right direction, before his owner had even committed to it. Dogs are needy. Oscar could never be that man, could never be a parent.

Charlotte took him to the beach when he was younger. Bournemouth, where an old aunt of hers was dying in a home. She must've been somewhere in her late forties at the time, but she still played in the sand with him. They made Hollywood film stars instead of castles, battled the wind in a game of tennis. Threw the ball back and forth, like this man with the dog. Except they were both inept, so the sight was laughable. Then she lay on the towel, scribbling into a journal, as he splashed about in the water. All she'd ever wanted was a child. There had been men in the picture, lovers in retrospect, but it wasn't a husband Charlotte had been auditioning. It was a father for her future son. Most of his life she'd been a tool for him, a tap for undivided love. And you only notice a tool when it stops working, and begrudge it for letting you down.

The trees around him are bare. Did autumn ever happen? All the red and gold leaves that dazzle him on an annual basis, where did they go? There must've been no colours this year, a result of global warming or something. A clump of leaves sticks to his shoe, a whole bunch of them, once green, then burning bright, now squashed down to a pulpy brown mass.

Everything's disposable.

Everybody.

In those moments he idolised Terry, from the seat next to him in a darkened cinema, the light of the screen on his face, the thought would've stung. Even when their romance started to rot, the meaningless things Terry did — the way his feet crossed over each other when they had to stand on the tube, his habit of scratching the bridge of his nose — were like museum artefacts to Oscar. But the past few weeks have made him face something. Humans are cold. Brutal. Blunt as beheading. Terry's coldness had a method. When Oscar said he lived in Kensington, he lost a point in his boyfriend's estimation. Another two when he expressed no interest in gaming or comic cons. Another when he didn't know Cornwall had its own language. A boyfriend got whittled down from a tree to a sapling to a twig that could break under a foot.

Even Oscar's been known to cut people out of his life with no damage done — Lauren and Andy, his first foster parents, or the couple of kids who spoke to him in school. It hurt like hell when Terry left, but not for long. Must've been the same afternoon of that limp goodbye when Oscar took out his phone and erased every text. Typed the boy's name into his e-mail search and deleted all those messages too. A pissed-off gardener, yanking out weeds.

But the process needs no action. If he were parted from Charlotte, he'd live. Without the voice recorder app on his phone, he'd sing. Without his voice, he wouldn't. Without an invite from Bella, days would still turn into nights.

Without Tim, he'll live.

Once in a while, it would be nice if Tim was walking in the street and saw something that triggered Oscar in his brain. Another Creole whackjob, chatting to herself on a bench. A simple time-out to appreciate someone who's a person enough, on his own terms, to be a part of his life.

Because it's all about you after all. Selfish prick. Because infatuation is an ego trip. The idea that a separate body can hurt you by doing nothing — if they don't text when you want them to, or are simply gone from the room. The desire to be desired, to be put first. When they leave, it's not their leaving that cuts deep, but the damage it's done to you. The deprivation of what pleased you. Ego, ego, ego.

Go listen to a sad song and say you relate. Go tweet about it. It's You vs. Everybody Else, every second you're alive. And Everybody Else is disposable.

Bits of Terry withered and fell away. When Tim came along, Terry got stamped to smithereens. Gone like yesterday. Until he came back to inflict more pain with a single glare. *Knob'ead*. May he go back to Tokyo and many a geisha trample his scrawny back.

And Charlotte. Hers is the biggest ego. Couldn't land a husband, couldn't have a kid, fostered one instead. Gave him cash and the figurehead on it, took away his choice. In a hundred years she, and her books, will be nothing but dust.

Where are you? C. Xx

The text is still flashing on his screen, the missed calls. He should leave her hanging, worried for his life.

No.

This is the ego trip, wanting to hurt Charlotte, and it's a cruelty he assumed he was incapable of. He has to respond to her.

She's the only one who's ever loved him.

A part of the city where buildings stand around grey and sad like used cartons. But his feet plough on until the sign comes into view. BRICK LANE, after all these months. The long stretch that starts out a great place for a mean pashmina before turning into rockabilly heaven at the top. Where Maya sits with a colleague in that jeweller's, surrounded by earrings of teapots and dice and vintage burlesque dancers. The thought of her comforting presence is tempting, but she'd sense his mood in a heartbeat. She'd prise open that can of worms, and nobody has the stamina to face that.

A man is led out of a shop by his large stomach, rotund as a pregnant lady's, to the point where it looks soldered onto the rest of his body. He arranges saris on a rail, prices them with tags from a plastic bag. Thick textured fabrics with peach patterned flowers, oceans of red. Mint green and salmon, streams of gold.

Dahl in the air. The cardamom mixes with the warning of rainfall, rain that'll frost to ice. A guy in a black shirt stands outside a restaurant, man-boobs sadly hanging. He squints into the light — grey, startling — as he invites passers-by in. *Best curry in town!* says every sign in every place.

'We're just looking,' says a man, speaking for himself and the thing on his arm. Both are tight in the face from smiling. She looks rigid as a bollard.

People have begun to trickle down towards him. Their chatter fills the streets like the litter at their feet. Strongbow cans kicked back and forth in an accidental match between shoes. At the Truman Brewery, the crowd thickens. People are no longer individuals, but one big glob of molasses heading towards him.

Ambient electronica, coming from who-knows-where, the man with the stall selling T-shirts maybe.

A girl in sweatpants walks by, talking on her phone. Something about a friend of hers and the cops. 'Just another dead nigga to them, bruv.'

A guy across the street takes photos of a bin with his phone. The bin is overflowing with rubbish, a volcano of trash. Styrofoam cups, bottles, cans, half-eaten kebabs, flyers, postcards, scrunched-up paper, receipts… The guy has a slight belly, thinning hair. He takes a photo as a girl in sunglasses tries to balance her own empty can on top of the pile, and he takes another photo as her can falls, to her mild panic, down to the hollowed-out pineapples on the pavement.

The sound of running feet. A boy is being chased down a side-street by other boys. Their shouts clash in the air, ricochet around the buildings and their victim's gasping body when they catch him up. The people who've noticed look around. Some walk towards the fuss, apprehensive but brave.

No way could Oscar do that. He couldn't face the sight of someone being killed. No-one can save these kids. They live to see each other dead.

It's only once he's in Kensington, out of the tube, drenched in sweat and rain, that his phone recovers enough signal to flash some new texts. Maybe it's Tim.

It isn't.

I'm so sorry, Osky. I should've told you.

The other one's from Charlotte. Woman texts like she's writing telegrams.

At Xandra and Alec's. All want to see you. C. Xx

The disappointment bristles. Bella has nothing to apologise for. But if that's the case, then why is there a lump in his throat?

Nothing stopped him from running out of Lukas' flat, back into those streets of Clapham without a clue, where this time even the foxes had no time for his pansy self. Bella deserves a text back, an apology. At the very least an explanation. Not that he could offer one.

As for Charlotte, she should be at home, waiting for him. But it's better that she isn't.

The soles of his shoes struggle on the black ice, succeed, but there comes the odd slide, the sudden jerk. His body's doing all the work, doesn't even need to think about righting itself. The ground is so frozen his feet will have to be amputated. Oh well. He'll have to do without them.

Back at the flat, his head swims with potential replies to Charlotte's text. Catty. Snotty. Angry. Self-righteous. Wounded. Martyred. She's betrayed him. His drowsiness has ebbed. The coffee is percolating and his voice, shakier than it used to be, rises from the depths of his gut.

At first it's a wail.

Then it finds a shape, and softens, moulds itself around melodies he's actually heard. *Nobody's Fault But Mine. River, Stay Away From My Door.*

It won't stop. Song after song gushes out of him, Tim's voice in his ear, complimenting him. Tim's swooping nose, eyes on his lips, and Charlotte, her delicate form, bones as slender as horsehair. She holds him tightly, every time she pulls him close. A strength that comes out of nowhere. Like those Amazon boas wrapping their kill.

Her bedroom door is open. So much space to search. The curtains are drawn, but the darkness suits him fine. The shapes of the bedside tables and the Habitat lamps, on either side of the double bed that only ever takes her weight, hers alone for all these years, a knot undone last night when she lifted the duvet for Tim. There's nothing to discover here, everything's out in the open. A long blonde hair in the cushions of the turquoise tub chair. A tiny scratch on the rose glass vase she squealed over in Selfridges. Intricate woven bookmarks in the middles of a whole stack of books. Christina Rossetti, Rumi, *The Power of Now, Gone Girl, An Unquiet Mind.* The host of perfumes on her dresser — Comme des Garçons, Jo Malone, L'Artisan Parfumeur. A tube of Elizabeth Arden cream. But it's in the bedsheets, the cotton, where the answer is waiting. In the waves of the sheets, something aquatic, old and sweet. Salted caramel, a sugared sea. And the proof that didn't need to be found.

Tim.

It's a punch in the throat.

Oscar's body labours for breath. In the process it exerts itself, makes itself gag, and pant, and heave. Nothing comes, other than his body's constant reaching. Coffee's brewed and waiting in the kitchen. Charlotte's at Xandra's, with that smug fucking Alec, bemoaning youths and urchins, sipping wine or sherry, checking her phone. She'll call. Tim's with her. Or not. He's with friends in a pub, or reading new work, or gone up to the Midlands already, to his family for Christmas. Must be midnight already. Or only five. It's so hard to tell in the winter.

The last time he saw Terry was the last time he cried. There had been enough signs, and there had been a lot of talk about it. But it was always *one day,* or *soon,* until it was finally *tomorrow*. And, on a dull grey day in June, *today*.

Condensation at the window. Kept him glued as Terry moved left to right and right to left in front of it, packing his stuff. Oscar didn't look at the suitcase on the bed. But he heard fabrics falling onto fabrics. The sound of an iPhone charger being yanked from its socket. Every now and then the phone would buzz, and Terry would stop to read the farewell texts from their friends. People who once shared a sofa and a drink with Oscar, who would never see him again. None except Maya and Lukas and Bella.

Terry grabbed his trunks from the radiator, unleashed for a brief, lingering moment that warm damp smell. Was he in such a hurry to leave? Their words lay unspoken, the entire afternoon a pause. 'I want to see you off,' Oscar had mumbled earlier when he called, to which the response on the other end of the line had been, 'Why?' Now Terry's anger — resentment? Sadness? — bullied him into silence.

Whatever Japan had in store for Terry, Oscar was lacking it. He'd come to argue a hopeless case. What was so special about Asia? Everybody thinks they know what a Thai ladyboy is and everybody loves Tokyo. Vietnam gap years, teaching English in China. Terry had a manner about him, every time he told someone his favourite films were by Studio Ghibli, that made Oscar cringe. He was leaving his boyfriend to prove he was a person. That he was an anime-loving homo with a sense of adventure. Fuck Chelsea, fuck Mayfair, fuck London. Climbing Mount Fuji to Cibo Matto in his ears. You can't talk about your boyfriend at the pub and expect a slap on the back. No-one gives a shit, or if they do it's the wrong kind. But they might listen if you said this crazy ex insisted on seeing you off, even though he was the last person on Earth you wanted to see. And while you were busy packing your suitcase for a gap year in Asia, the entire continent, your boyfriend —ex— was staring at the condensation in the window, silent, until that old vague sadness overcame him, brought tears to his eyes.

'Terry, don't leave.'

It wasn't even a sentence. More an odd noise that could have been lost in the folding of clothes. But Terry turned as if his iPad had exploded. That look on his face. Pure hatred.

'I'm sorry. I didn't mean to say that.'

That was true. It'd been the most exercise he'd ever done, keeping those feelings locked in. But now he'd have to live with that pitiful outburst, relive it, and what it did to Terry's face. He only hardened when Oscar's tears ran.

'I'm going to miss you. I'm sorry.'

Oscar's hands wiped his tears away, but they kept running.

'I'll miss you, I'm sorry,' while Terry quickened his pace.

'I'll miss you,' with the sound of the zip shutting the suitcase.

Terry stood, finished. 'I told you not to come.' He turned off the heating and looked about him. Nothing on the radiators. 'Come on,' he said, taking Oscar by the elbow and leading him to the door. 'Let's get to the tube.'

At the station, there was no kiss. No goodbye hugs and no more crying. Terry raised his hand, looking the other way. Then he slapped his Oyster card on the barrier and made for the escalator. He sank into the shadows of the station. Oscar was left alone outside, unable to follow.

He couldn't walk right, or even at all for a few minutes.

But at least the crying had stopped.

The pile of books on Charlotte's bedside-table is too neat. Looks pretty in the dark, the edges of the stacked tomes outlined in a pale blue. The freestanding clock on the dresser ticks. His phone buzzes in his pocket. The vibrations snake from his leg to the mattress to the pillow to his head. Must be Charlotte calling. But it's hard to keep his eyelids open.

This is where Tim lay, where he rested his head.

One of the books in the pile is called *Understanding Depression*. The phone continues to buzz. What does Charlotte have to be depressed about? Must be research material. Some shite about a shirtless artist with anxiety. A randy housewife with a complex. But before the resentment has a chance to grow, the numbness takes hold.

This is where Tim fell asleep. Where the same will happen to Oscar, if he doesn't get himself up.

11 A BIG COAT

He wakes up to find an arm around him. Charlotte's. Her mouth hangs open, breath rustling along the roof of her mouth, and she stirs when he gets up. He should've cleared out last night. She and Tim must've got back eager for nookie, only to find Oscar like a passed-out Effie Gray on their shag-mat. The shame of it.

No Carolina. Must be Sunday again. As the coffee gets going in the kitchen, he searches the flat for Tim. The man isn't on the settee, or out on the balcony smoking. It hits him that Charlotte might've put him in Oscar's room, in his bed. The door creaks open. Tim might be there, waking up naked in his bed. He'll sit up straight, duvet sliding off him, and suppress a yawn as he wishes Oscar good morning.

But there's nobody there. Not a trace of him in the room, not that scent of his on the sheets or the pillowcase. Just a musty odour. He opens the window for the air to sweep the room. It's freezing today. He thinks to cover himself but it looks as though he's already dressed. In the same clothes he wore to the restaurant. The tramp.

'Morning, darling.'

Charlotte's standing at the kitchen door, dressing gown and tumbling hair. He's never been up before her.

'I didn't mean to fall asleep,' he says. It came out before he could stop it.

'Oh, it's alright. You must've been tired.' And she's smiling at him as if nothing weird had happened at all. 'Get ready, though. I thought it'd be nice to have a day out together.'

So that's it. She's going to lure him out and dump him at an orphanage.

They have breakfast together with Radio 4 in the background, and an empty seat where Tim ought to be.

An hour-and-a-half later, the cab drops them off by the Waldorf in Aldwych. Charlotte claims she has nothing smaller than a fifty, and tells the cabbie to keep the change. She takes her almost-son by the arm, looking fetching in a mint-green cardigan, and leads him around the Novello and up Catherine Street. She's trying to please him. She wants him to feel fuzzy, to swoon over sights such as Hope & Greenwood on the corner, red-and-white stripes adorned with garlands. Toffees and sugar mice, jars of humbugs, rhubarb and custard sweets, lemon bonbons and candy canes enough to make a child pass out from joy. She's trying so hard it pains him, to the point where he wants to stop and tell her enough's enough. He's too jaded for this shit.

On the approach to the Piazza, the smell of roasting meat in the air. Ale, mixing with the drizzle. December, and still no goddamn snow. The Piazza is buzzing, crowds drifting between the columns to buy bracelets and brooches and cameos, antique binoculars and kaleidoscopes, or standing in large groups to watch the street performers. The gold-painted living statues, the headless man, the dancers and magicians that dazzle tourists. Someone's being a floating Yoda, but has clearly never seen or heard Yoda.

And when it couldn't get more of a handjob, there's a line of people, waiting in queue to stroke a couple of real-live reindeer. Charlotte is a bubbling wreck at the sight of them. She pulls Oscar into the queue and keeps looking ahead to check their progress. When it's their turn to stroke the deer, her eyes are perfect circles. These are reindeer, right in front of them. These strange beasts with the rough-tender hair, and the antlers that aren't plastic or foam or stuffed with wool. How weird everything is. Weird, because there's no other word for it. This exists in his universe, this big, muscular creature with the snout and the studded reins they make it wear. One of the deer is lazy, lowers himself to the ground. The other shifts his weight, the hooves scraping against the cobbles. Charlotte is entranced. Her hand strokes the standing one's head, feels its every hair. This is happiness, mixed with wonder, and sadness, a twinge of fear.

Then it's over, the path cleared for the family of five behind them. Charlotte can't accept the separation, keeps flicking her eyes back even as she heads for the church.

Inside it, the atmosphere is buzzing. Men, women, old-timers and young'uns gather beneath the chandeliers and the high ceiling. Rain in the stained-glass windows, middle-aged women of a comfortable size offering mince pies and mulled wine to the congregation. Relief ceiling and alcoves, lined with gold. Columns at the altar, but that's about it. None of the madness of Hagia Sophia in Istanbul. No whirling Dervishes. And no Virgin Mary statues, bleeding from the eyes, or morbid icons. No Jesus, ripped and spiked, dying on a cross.

Only a host of angel voices, singing from the altar.

A thrill of hope, the weary world rejoices…

The notes climb higher up the ceiling, the echoes falling down on them.

Fall on your knees… !

A chill to the marrow. As the song soars, Charlotte's lips part, her eyes watering. A woman in the row behind them has shut her eyes — or rather, the song has shut them. As if an invisible hand's passed over her face.

Oscar remembers a story Bella told him, about a church off the Strand somewhere, sometime in the nineteenth century. A priest who sold more crypt space than was actually possible. Taking money from the poor while flushing their loved ones down the open sewers into the Thames. He can't help thinking it, even though he shouldn't. Not here. If the congregation could read his mind, these moved and beautiful souls, he'd be ex-communicated. Stoned to death.

He should contact Bella, apologise.

A few moments later, the youngish priest takes the altar. He adopts a light tone as he reminds everyone of the true meaning of Christmas. There was no X-Box in the manger, he jokes, nor a *Doctor Who* special to look forward to after dinner. Just a young mother, a humble carpenter and their miracle baby. And all of a sudden, for the first time in Oscar's life, they're people. Real people. Mary, Joseph and Jesus, like many before them. Mary holds a baby she's too young to care for. Almond eyes, a challenge in her stare. Joseph is a man, older than her, trying to do right. Jesus, a strange boy who grew up to be a superstar, his antics twisted into myth. And thousands of years later, here they are, and here he is, in a room with a hundred bowed heads and closed eyes.

Drip by drip, fear gathers inside him. *God is in the gaps*. It repeats in his head. His stomach grows cold and Charlotte is a different woman. Nothing's familiar. All around him are somnambulists, laughing at the preacher's words, colluding for the amens. It unsettles him. He's wandered into another tribe, hoping he won't be caught.

After the priest's speech, a TV actor contributes his bit. Scattered applause from those who know him. He reads a passage from Corinthians:

When I was a child, I spake as a child, I understood as a child, I thought as a child: but when I became a man, I put away childish things.

For now we see through a glass, darkly, but then face to face. Now I know in part, but then shall I know even as also I am known.

Charlotte is amazed. Oscar, too. But she isn't his mother and he isn't her son.

After the service, Charlotte insists on dropping by Trafalgar Square to see the tree. 'It's tradition!' she says in a sing-song voice. She sets off towards the Tesco on the corner, turns down New Row. Her book's on display in the Waterstones window, which she greets with a small laugh. There's a lady selling Big Issues, which Charlotte politely declines while handing her a fiver. Then it's St Martin's Lane, Starbucks and Nero, Prêt in the distance, fundraisers with donations buckets all around. St Martin-in-the-Fields, imposing as a duke, across the road from the Square.

At the front of the National Gallery, a soldier in a wheelchair sings from *Miss Saigon,* while across from him a man in a top hat plays a tuba that breathes fire. The flames shock the passers-by, but they laugh and toss handfuls of coins into the tuba case.

'Do you remember when I first brought you here?' Charlotte says, and stops them to admire the Christmas tree. 'You were terrified of the pigeons. Remember what it was like, when the place was full of them? But then I pointed out a poor little one that had lost a foot, and you smiled when you saw him walk along undeterred. Poor little thing, on his stump. After that, you let them all flock to you. We bought a bag of seeds from a vendor and they all came flying. Remember that?'

There's even a photo of him, giving his best Mariah Carey to the Pentax as he's besieged by hungry beaks. 'Yeah… That was lovely.'

Teens in quilted jackets and Gap scarves take photos of Tuba Guy, and they cheer as the flames burst out of his instrument. They look Italian. Italy—- another place he's never been to. Charlotte is the sort of person who likes nothing better than to stroll around Kew Gardens. She spent almost an hour entranced by a teapot shop off New Bond Street last year, was only moved along by the promise of fabrics at Liberty. She knows every line of the national anthem, has the TV ready every Christmas at three o'clock for the Queen's speech. Exuded an air of personal shame whenever Harry made the front pages of tabloids. William's engagement was a heartening turn of events, after the student riots, and the wedding was the perfect happy ending. When others talk of exotic adventures in Marrakech or Mozambique, Charlotte pirouettes the conversation to her stay in the Cotswolds, the gorgeous Yorkshire cottage she found on Airbnb, or the breathtaking views of the Peak District. Our country may be small, she says, but look how much it packs into its tiny frame.

'Charlotte…' he says.

She turns, startled but pleased, because she doesn't know what's coming. She's spurred him onto this.

That's what this is, a reaction. He mustn't feel guilty.

'What do you know about my real mother?'

That's all it takes to wipe the smile off her face. Her lips part to reveal the small gap in her teeth. Like the chip in Tim's. A few feet away, some waif starts to sing *Silent Night*, a beardy man with a harp as her backing track. Charlotte struggles to find the right expression. At last she says, 'Not much, I'm afraid. It's natural that you should want to know about her, you have every right to know, but I'm sorry, Oscar, really. There's nothing we can know about her for sure.'

Muffled applause behind them. What's been dormant all these years in the back of his head finally comes to the forefront. 'You mean I was… found.' His voice came out brittle, more wounded than it should have.

'Yes,' she says.

'Not given.'

'No.'

Charlotte looks relieved and afraid at the same time. The lights on the Christmas tree hang straight downwards. Someone hung them up in vertical lines, no swoops, not the least bit of romance in the design.

'Before Lauren and Andy,' Charlotte continues, 'you were with another couple, but they proved to be… incapable. She wasn't your real mother, if you remember that lady. You used to remember her, anyway. You used to mention her sometimes. Kate. Remember? I thought you believed her to be your real mum so I let that be. But I'm afraid no-one knows who your actual mother was.' She stops herself, but something tells her to go on. 'However, they did suspect a girl. She was homeless, and hung around outside the Barnardo's in Brixton. She used to wear a big coat— But… no-one knew for certain.'

So it wasn't his mother who'd named him.

'I'm sorry,' Charlotte says. 'Truly. I wouldn't wish for any child—'

His cheeks are hot. The child in him wants to run, punch the singing waif, throw her face into Tuba Flames, kick Beardy Man's harp over. Run into the gallery and hide under a Rembrandt. But none of it would amount to anything. There's no need for all that drama.

Charlotte grips his arm. 'I wanted a child,' she says. 'I found you. And you found me.'

She means it. The wrinkles on her cold face, and her lips, pink and thin and trembling. How can he break her heart? To hurt her is to drown a kitten. She's fragile. A good Christian. He mustn't break her heart.

'I'm glad you found me.'

It was the right thing to say. Makes her laugh, half-laugh and half-cry, and then she puts her hand on his cheek. Caresses it. She was fourteen years younger when she saved him, when she was looking for someone to love. A silence falls between them. Around them is the noise of kids and distant singing, people knocking on the iced water of the fountains.

It's like someone's pressing down on his chest. That man in New York, held by the cops — *I can't breathe*. Some people have real problems. Oscar's lucky and it's time he knew it. His life is one big privilege.

Charlotte begins to speak, but her voice comes out grainy. She clears her throat and starts again. 'I was thinking of inviting Tim to our place,' she says. 'A sort of pre-Christmas celebration before he travels up to his family. What do you think?'

Tim in a jumper, sipping mulled wine by the tree.

'Yeah. Yeah, that's nice.'

She contemplates him. 'Good,' she says. 'It'll be fun.'

The glow of the tree lights, the singer's voice wavering in the wind. Charlotte is so English sometimes, all niceties and euphemisms. Instead of saying, *I want to be with my boyfriend,* she phrased it as though they were having a tea party. Like when they used to say pregnant chicks were *in the family way*. It's also clear she admits the value of Tim between them. This Christmas, his presence is necessary, in a way that no-one else's ever was before. This year, he's the only thing they have in common.

Charlotte's eyes, wet and blinking, are on the tree in the square. Tourists pose in front of it. A woman with mad, frizzy hair, tiny black shades. Something about her says Dutch. Funny how you learn to tell.

'It's heartwarming, isn't it?' Charlotte says, meaning the tree. 'That the Norwegians send it every year? Such a sweet gesture.'

And she's right, it is sweet. A good ol' Yuletide story that somehow came to be, and continues to be. Probably 'til long after everyone here in the Square is dead.

Don't you want to find your mother? Terry would ask. *Aren't you even curious?* And during the time he was with Oscar, the answer was no. Charlotte was enough. Why chase someone who doesn't want you, when you've all the love you need? But this wasn't the right response. Terry's forehead would crease, his affection withdraw. For the rest of the day, he'd be as distant as a stranger on the tube. He'd dismiss any idea of Oscar's as fantasy, any observation as error. Oscar's opinions became monitored, kept under curfew, until they were too afraid to come out.

Now here he is, a boy with knowledge of his birth-mother. Lady was a tramp, literally. She roamed the streets like her son, was the same pointless twat he is. She wore a big coat, that much is known. Probably not a Karen Millen, and probably not a big furry number out of *Dr Zhivago*. On the way past a vintage clothing shop, an old army trench coat catches his eye. That's the one. If his mother's going to be homeless, she can at least look bad-ass. Chilblains on her knuckles, fag behind her ear, knife in her boot. A dab hand at lighting a fire. Crouching over a barrel for the warmth of its flames, singing songs in a different language.

It's a thought that came to him sometime in the night, that maybe his mother wasn't even English. It would explain his feeling of constant exclusion. Oscar's always regarded his supposed homeland as though he's only read about it. A landscape of gentle undulations, still clouded by the mists of battle. A Mother for which apple-cheeked Tommys fought. A country of brown leather shoes, tea towels, Marmite and pillboxes. It only takes a street sign to evoke nostalgia for a world that may never have existed. Primrose Hill. Petticoat Lane. Cock Lane, the prozzies or the rooster fights. Horseferry Road. St Bride. Blackfriars. Gipsy Hill, named so that everybody knew what sort of person travelled there. England is a thousand-year-old Queen Bitch who thunders in to tear the party up. Invade, stir and leave. To plant mines and stand well back as the locals wander into the blast radius. Congrats, Your Majesty, you birthed Shakespeare and the Beatles. Big Ben? Genius. The Tower of London? Poor princes, great story. Brings those snap-happy tourists in. The Twenty-Twelve Olympics, the London Eye and poppies. St George's Cross, Crusaders and football rage and chavs. North and South. Almost as bad as India and Pakistan. England, what have you done? Get another Shakespeare. Wash that dirt out of your hair, filthy rivers down the plughole. Bodies down the Thames. The hills of London are piles of corpses, victims of the Plague. And people lose their shit over John Lewis Christmas ads.

'Oh look,' says Bella, 'an HSBC. We should probably grab some dough.' And she links arms with him to cross the road. She smiles as though she won something beautiful. 'How sad is this? I'm back to needing pocket money from my mum.'

'I always have.'

Bella laughs. 'I'd divorce mine if I could, the swine. Trouble is, we both like a nice cup of tea and Radio 4.'

Sounds like Charlotte. Maybe they should meet.

In Oscar's bank account there's an extra two grand. Charlotte opens her purse even wider at Christmas. This is it, his legacy.

Monthly deposits from a foster mother, received without so much as a crease of the forehead. Every check of his balance should be a shock to his system. And those numbers have only got bigger since he forgot how to spend. Eight-thousand pounds one day, nine-thousand another, twelve, seventeen... An idea works its way around his head, *Give it all away*. Well, why not? What use is it to him, when the very idea of buying anything seems pointless? He ends up with hundreds of pounds in his back pocket, waiting for an East-End homeboy to rescue them and give them a good home. Waiters and buskers will get two-hundred percent tips from now on.

Yet somehow, Charlotte, Charlotte, Charlotte, the money will keep coming back. How can he even think of leaving her, without a job and no worth? When somewhere out there is a girl, too afraid to check her bank balance, without a job or future, or parents at all. Queuing for a pack of biscuits at the food bank, or a can of beans. Nothing on her but a big coat.

They've done the market up all Christmassy, garlands coiled around pillars, railings and staircases. Chinese grandmas sell Michael Jackson T-shirts and schoolbags. (The King's been dead five years, Diana even longer.) Hand luggage made of yellow newsprint. Stalls of jewellery and knick-knacks, shirts, military hats and boxes of records. It reminds him of Rough Trade, and the amount of time it's been since he last went to buy a record. He was even on Brick Lane the other day, and it never occurred to him to go.

Finally, at a random stall, the idea comes to him. The perfect gift for Tim is lying here in wait. Boxes of old photos, laid out on the table for him to flick through. A puff of old chemicals unleashed with every one. There are gems here. One of a couple, standing on a beach in the Twenties or Thirties, looking in different directions. One of a man with a pipe in his mouth, riding a horse. There's got to be one like it somewhere, until at last it appears.

An old lady in a hat, sitting on a bench. His and Tim's Creole nutjob.

A sudden shame descends on him. Why 'nutjob'? Because the woman felt the need to speak to someone? What does it matter that no-one was there?

'So cool!' Bella gasps. She touches the photo as if it were an icon. 'We're such hipsters it's not even funny.'

But she has no idea what he's doing this for, and the secrecy makes him flush. This photo, stuck in a simple black album, with a caption in Pidgin French. *Non joué on le grass!* Perfect. A bunch of these pictures, people and made-up stories, and a book to stick them in. Some funky wrapping paper for the man to tear open. Present it in a box, for extra tease.

Tim will be with them for a pre-Christmas celebration. Oscar's throat feels tight at the thought of it.

When they sit for a coffee, confession's on the tip of his tongue. It almost comes out when Bella talks about Lukas, their up-and-down thing that's been going on for months. Her eyes are on the steaming drink, a half-eaten cake cast aside. 'I already know it'll never work,' she says. 'That's what the Norwegian guy was about, I suppose. A way of cutting free.'

'Why wouldn't it work?' His desire to know intensifies with her silence. If she can give him this, if only this, to work with...

'Because, looking at it from a bird's-eye view, it simply doesn't. We're not a good match. He'd annoy me with his casualness and he'd be dismissive of my neuroses, which would only make me more neurotic. That's more a recipe for a buddy cop movie than a romance.'

A boy in an apron comes to take the empty cups left on the table. Bella hands him the rest of her cake with a smile, pats her stomach to show it had been too much for her.

The boy gone, she picks up where she left off. 'I know it seems clinical of me, and maybe it's those neuroses talking, but I think love — the kind that lasts — is a thing more practical than passionate. If the pieces fit together, the whole is less likely to topple over, right?' She sips, then meets his eye. 'Look. I've liked Lukas since we were thirteen. That's a lot of time, a lot of emotion. But there's carrying a torch, and there's flogging a dead horse. Right now I interest him, but two months from now he'll grow bored and find a thinner, whiter girl.'

'But maybe not.' The photos for Tim's gift sit wrapped in a paper bag on the table. The thought of laying the man to rest makes Oscar's throat close up again. The key is that he and Tim are a good match. It's easy. The pieces fit together. Even if the words that stick in his head are *straight* and *bent*.

—•—

Tim, I've got to tell you something. Something you probably already know, but that doesn't make it any easier. The first time I saw you at the book launch, I was intrigued. But then my feelings… developed from there. So what I'm saying is, I like you. I know, I shouldn't, but there it is. You came into my life and I fell for you. For your stories, and your… effect. Ever since you told me that story about the Evil Eye, I can't get you out of my head. I know you're with Charlotte, and I know how pointless this is but I only wanted to let you know. That you're the first thought in someone's head, every day. That you matter to someone. You happened to him and he's glad you did.

All day, the speech has been going around in his mind like a prayer. Tonight he'll give it.

It's the morning of faux-Christmas and it's stopped raining. But the sky's too cloudy for snow. There's still hope for the evening, when he and Tim are sitting by the lit-up tree, chatting, the darkened room lit by a flurry of silent falling flakes in the window. Stranger things have happened.

For now, there's the faux-Christmas meal, prepared by Carolina and served up by an insistent Charlotte. A turkey with pear and pecan stuffing. Cranberry-and-orange sauce, roast potatoes, sprouts, honey-roasted parsnips, dips and croutons and grissini. Three choices of dessert. Christmas Cake, light on brandy, heavy on fruit. Pudding. And, best of all, home-made toffee apples. Charlotte's gone to town (or rather, made Carolina go).

Tim leads the toast and they all raise their glasses to clink when he's finished. Later on he entertains them with accurate renditions of Top Forty hits. Charlotte spasms with giggles, covering her mouth as her eyes clamp shut, thrilled by her boyfriend's performance.

Oscar doesn't want the night to come. Not yet.

Charlotte offers tea, and puts the kettle on to get the Earl Grey brewing. In-between the pleasant hot sips, they exchange and unwrap their gifts to each other, by the little fir tree she spent the whole of yesterday evening decorating. She gasps like a younger woman at her gift from Oscar, a hand-carved mirror. Such fine handiwork, it must be German, she reasons. Or Swiss. So delicate and sturdy, so finely honed.

She then gives Oscar his gift, the paper of which is so expertly stuck down it highlights his lack of exercise. But finally, the paper relents.

A microphone.

'I want you to promise me,' she says, 'that you'll start singing again.'

Like putting him in front of a ship's wheel and yelling, *TO AMERICA!* But it touches him all the same.

'What with that and your Logic Pro,' Tim says, 'You've got a home studio.'

So that's what she meant by the Logic Pro on the anniversary Macbook.

'Thank you, it's great.' The comment is barely a whisper, muffled by Charlotte's jumper as she hugs him. Tim knew all about this. Charlotte whispered her plans to him, months in advance, and they've been counting down the days for him to be a real boy again.

'You should hear him sing,' she says, beaming at Tim. 'The priest wanted him in the choir when he was younger, but he was too shy. He has a marvellous voice.'

'I could tell.'

And there's another moment, a stillness where the man smiles at him and their eyes stay locked.

Tonight. It needs to happen tonight.

'Alright, darling,' Charlotte interrupts, handing Tim a parcel. 'It's time for you to open yours now!'

He turns his head, and it's like a boy's too. Somewhat big for its frame, but delicately made. He tears apart the wrapping to be met with three cashmere sweaters. All of them perfect, the right choice for his colouring. He kisses Charlotte as thanks, a quick peck, and puts one of the sweaters on over his shirt. A brown one, toffee, to match his eyes.

Now it's time for Oscar's gift to him. 'You didn't have to get me anything,' Tim says, accepting the parcel. Charlotte's put a CD of choral music on, the King's College choir, and the sound of tearing paper is like distortion in the harmonies. The paper is too silly. The ribbons and bows excessive. The gift is shit. Humiliating. What if Tim misunderstands, thinks Oscar is mocking the lady in the park instead of hero-worshipping her? The blood rushes to his face. If only he could take it back, before Tim even sees it. Before Charlotte understands and it's all too late.

But when he holds the album in his hands, Tim's eyes light up. The moment he sees the first captioned photo, he gets it. The surprised glee on his face. Charlotte narrows her eyes at the gift, turns from Tim to Oscar. Her colour changes.

'Thank you,' Tim says. 'This is really... brilliant.'

His smile shrinks a little, and he puts his hand on Charlotte's back. She breathes out. There's a world going on in that boy's head of his, a thousand mental processes that Oscar would be able to read if he could only look long enough. But he shouldn't, not while Charlotte is in the room. Best thing to do is keep a low profile. Downplay, and look away.

'Merry Christmas,' Tim says, and hands Oscar his gift.

A white box. Inside it is a black Bible.

There's a brief moment of disappointment, which must register on his face, until it becomes clear what language it's in.

Creole.

Tim is pleased, can't stop himself grinning.

Oscar flicks to a random page, reads the foreign English. *Jiizas–di buk we Luuk rait bout im.* Renders him speechless. And its effect is one neither of them could've seen coming. This book is more than just a perfect gift from the perfect man, more even than the one, insignificant, silly in-joke they share. It's bigger than the two of them. It's what it says about the woman chatting to herself in the park. A history, a world.

'You like it, then?' Tim says, already knowing the answer.

Charlotte gets up. 'Well, that's it for another year, darlings,' she says, scrunching up the wrapping paper and walking to the kitchen.

They spend the rest of the afternoon in front of the TV, as if it's Christmas for real. Tim says he half-expects Charlotte to have got a hold of the Queen's speech. To which she replies that she has, along with a request from Her Majesty for a signed copy of the next book. Then there's the tuning in and out of holiday movies, *Home Alone* and *A Muppet Christmas Carol,* Charlotte in stitches at Tim's obvious love of both. He teases her back about knowing the names of the meerkats in the adverts, and crying at penguins in love. They then pick at the tin of Quality Street while playing Scrabble, Tim enthusing about the Latitude festival a few summers ago where he saw The Irrepressibles, and promising to give Oscar their EP.

Charlotte's eyelids droop as the sun goes down. It's time for her to turn in, she says. Got to be up early for that jog, burn those faux-Christmas calories. 'Have a good Christmas,' she says to Tim. Oscar's head turns away out of politeness when they kiss, before she disappears into the dark corridor. A moment later, her door shuts. Oscar's stomach goes cold.

So Tim isn't spending the night. Half of Oscar is relieved to be left alone with him, the other half petrified. It's been months, weeks, all day, and now the time has come. He can't let Tim get away. Not yet.

But Tim doesn't want to go anywhere. 'I'm tired of this Christmas shit,' he says, and turns off the choral music now that it's safe. 'Let's put on some PJ Harvey.'

So they do, all the lights switched off except for the tree's. The whole of *To Bring You My Love* groans and moans from the speakers like sex in a bayou. Tim is sitting next to Oscar on the sofa, his new brown jumper turned to caramel by the tree lights. He's facing Oscar, leaning towards him with one arm resting by the boy's shoulder.

'Do you spend Christmas alone, you two?'

'Pretty much. Sometimes we go to Alec and Xandra's, but they're in Scotland this year.'

'Not bad.'

There's a pause, waiting to be filled.

'My ex used to call her Belgravia. Xandra, I mean. That was his nickname for her.' Coward. Yellow-liver. Jessie.

Tim laughs, more out of politeness than anything.

'So you'll be with your parents?'

'Well… My dad's dead…'

'Oh yeah, sorry.'

Tim laughs, for real now. 'Don't be. But my mum and sister and brother-in-law and cousins are all up there, so it makes more sense if I go home, rather than try to cram everyone into my poky London flat.'

'Are you guys big on Christmas?'

Tim cringes, drowsy. 'Yeah… I s'pose we shouldn't be, right? At least, I shouldn't be. But, I don't know. Things change. Meanings change, I mean. You don't need to believe in Jesus to eat a turkey and be good to your fellow man, do ya?'

'Yeah…'

Tim, I like you.

They're close enough to kiss. Charlotte's in bed, Tim wants to stay here on the sofa, talking. To be with him.

I like you.

They're in his bedroom, a few minutes from now, unable to part their lips, the clothes falling at their feet.

They're in Covent Garden, five years from now, together and making dinner. Hosting their own Christmas parties. The idea would take some getting used to, but Charlotte would accept in the end that this was the right ending.

But then there's that other ending. He and Tim are at a function, decades from now. They've never been together, and Tim married someone else. A polite conversation between them, then he turns to some ginger infant and says, *Come on… OSCAR.*

In another ending, one of them dies. Tragipoetically, beautifully. The other is doomed to pine.

Oscar is tired, and the laughter spills out of him. It's all so stupid. Tim is here, alive, but with Charlotte. And it shouldn't be so. It shouldn't, but it is. The world is so fucked up, so much more than this, too. And the man looks confused as the giggles threaten to choke him. Maybe this is how Oscar dies. Laughing like a dunce at nothing, a handsome man left bewildered to deal with the mess.

'What's so funny?' says Tim. 'You're turning purple!'

'Nothing. It's not… It's not funny.' He's pissed as a duchess. Mulled bloody wine.

Tim exhales through his nose, smiles, to wrap the night up. 'Anyway…' He slides his arm away, rises from the sofa, joints clicking.

But he can't leave, not yet. 'Shall we put on another one?' Oscar jumps up to eject the CD. 'You choose.'

'I think we need to go to bed.'

A silence drops.

Tim came out with it. Just like that. The words buzz between them, refuse to fade. *Let's go to bed.*

But Tim is getting up and walking away.

Walking away.

'Goodnight, Oscar. Thanks for the gift. I really, really liked it.'

He's at the front door.

'Oh. Yeah. Same here. Goodnight.'

And then he's gone, leaving behind a warm seat and the smell of Fahrenheit on the sofa.

12 END OF THE LINE

A woman in her twenties boards the tube with a boy of a different skin tone. A guitar is strapped to her back and her hand grips the boy's. They both look over their shoulders every now and then, as though they're about to join a band or just escaped one. She's saved the boy. She's kidnapped him. Kid's a mute, Holly Hunter in *The Piano*.

He'll put this in a song. This, the woman and the boy on the District line. For no reason other than to put it in a song. If anybody asks, *What's the significance of it? Why's it even in there?* he'll say, *Fuck significance. It's there because it is.* Fancy that. In a crowd, amongst hipsters and travellers and Cityboys and others worse and better off than him, he could even be a songwriter.

First and foremost, he should leave Charlotte. He's got enough bread in the bank to go online and get himself a bachelor pad, get a flippin' job. Whatever it is. Someone will hire him, if he finds a joint with loose morals and tells the boss he's only sixteen. The thought excites him. Out of nowhere he can see himself, changed for the better, embarking on a whole new life. Picking out furniture for his new pad, the bed and the chairs and rugs. Make it his place, not Charlotte's. Wall-to-wall bookcases filled with records, posters of Cat Power and Patti Smith. *Rid of Me*. And he won't be sharing a flat with a bunch of wankers like Maya does, he'll live on his own. Or with Bella, if she's up for it.

But then Lukas would be over all the time. They'd have sex or fights in the next room. Whatever it is they've got, it's doomed to die. Bella saw it coming but also sees it going. When you're playing breakup songs at the start of the fling, there's no way it'll end in marriage. And Tim already told him that, through the mixtape. A song about getting drunk and horny in Mexico, followed by a guy looking for love. A chick mourning a dead romance. Brel begging a lover to stay, through a lungful of tar.

Charlotte and Tim will never last. They're right and left. As different from each other as gay and straight, and everything in-between. It'll only get worse as Tim gets angrier, less willing to sit back at the dinner-table and accept her privilege. He doesn't have the same ties to her as Oscar has. He isn't her son.

All the same, Oscar needs to leave Charlotte too. Find his real mother, get an explanation, build something. The girl in the coat who dumped him in Brixton was down and out. Homeless, reaching out to a charity to take her kid. But she left him without a word. Nobody knows who, or where, she is. Unless she makes contact first, there's no way he'll ever find her. Not in a city of eight million people. Not if she's dead. Because she could well be. Killed by a gang on the street. Killed by the snowfall he'd loved so much a few years back. One of those suicides holding up trains. Suits on the tarmac, coats on the tracks.

He and she are still connected somehow. By DNA, by memories flickering like candlelight inside him. Maybe she wasn't ginger. Maybe that came from his dad. She could have been a foreigner. Someone who believed in, wore, an Evil Eye.

She is who he takes after. She sang to him, huddled in alcoves and porticos. Roamed the city, with him in her arms. Fell in love with men who leave.

Without Charlotte's money to prop him up, Oscar would have ended up like her. Starved and broken, sleeping outside, all his yearning suppressed. Dreams are for the well-off, ideals for the old.

Off the escalator and out of the station, Oscar walks straight past the Witnesses waiting outside — three of them now — to a girl with a bobble-hat and clipboard, bright jacket glowing in the grey day. Her hands are shivering. She looks young, eighteen. Suddenly, eighteen is young to him.

'Hello!' she says, over the moon that somebody's stopped.

'I'd like to donate, please.'

She laughs. 'Well, that was easy! That's ace, thank you. I'll just talk you through the small print.' And she does. Reads things out about monthly payments, Direct Debit agreement, on and on, he isn't even listening. Just itching to put his mark on the dotted line.

When she hands him the clipboard, he freezes.

'Something wrong?' she says.

He looks from the paper to her jacket and back again. *Barnardo's.*

Someone's playing a joke. Next he'll be looking at the ground and the girl will say her grandma's dead. They like the same bands, she's looking for a flatmate, soon they'll be the best of friends. A shiver runs up his body and the hairs on his arms stand on end, but he's laughing. Beyond control. The girl looks worried for her life.

After a second, the laughter subsides. 'Sorry. I'm just— How much should I donate?'

'Oh, that's totally up to you. Some people pay two pounds a month, others pay ten, twenty. Obviously, the more the better.'

'So, like, two hundred ... ?'

He leaves the girl happier than he's ever made anybody, and there's a brighter tone in her voice as he walks away. More confidence as she says hello to all the strangers crossing the street to avoid her.

They've put Charlotte behind a low table in Classics, between Sci-Fi & Fantasy and the kids' section. Two members of staff adjust the black tablecloth and arrange the copies of the novel into neat piles. Behind Charlotte is a wall of Ws, emblazoned on seven feet of vinyl. The artwork for the book on it. *You're On!* Scripty font over a sassy sketch. A sophisticated woman wearing heels and headphones. There's a crease in the fabric, makes it look as though the chick's face has been punched from the inside. Two boys and an older lady stand behind the tills, watching the line of customers. Pre-signed copies of *You're On!* stacked neatly between them. They look at each other with meaning. One of the boys is like Terry, carbon copy, down to the V05 hair and silicone wristbands. The older lady's eyes dart from Charlotte to her queue of fans to her colleagues, and she raises an eyebrow, causing the boys to smirk. People always hate Charlotte, which makes Oscar want to protect her.

She greets every fan, women with pushchairs and students with aunty's Christmas wishlist in their pockets. They chat for a few seconds, she finds something to compliment them on, and she signs their book. Her denim'd legs squirm beneath the tablecloth. Her feet twist in their heels, grind into the carpet.

'Oscar,' she says, eyes wide, when she looks up. She lifts a hand up, *Hang on*. The publicist, straight fringe and a tartan scarf, leans in on cue to check what's up, and Charlotte whispers in her ear. They agree she needs a five-minute fag break.

Outside, in the unromantic backyard of the shop's delivery entrance, Charlotte digs out her vape-stick for a longed-for vape. Oscar doesn't need to smoke. His head's too clear, eyes alert. The freshness of the air is in his nostrils.

'So sweet of you to come, darling,' Charlotte says. 'Are you alright?'

'I like him.'

At last.

Charlotte looks confused, squints as she takes a puff at the surrogate smoke. And then, without his needing to say another word, it clicks. 'Tim?'

'Yeah.'

Something inside her bends. Her face sags, the brackets around her mouth deepen. He's finally hurt her and meant it. 'How long?'

'Since he came to the flat the first time, and he told me the Eye story.'

'What Eye story?'

'The Evil Eye.'

His hand goes to his collarbone, where the Eye sits snug under his clothes. He has half a mind to take it off, throw it into a bin, but the thought of it bruises his heart. A cat jumps onto a cardboard recycling bin, and his eyes well up. The tears run down his cheeks. His mouth is open, twitching. His mind whirrs, a zoetrope of thoughts that bring a lump to his throat. Tim, Terry, the Kiwi foster parents, Kate before them, his real mum, his hair, his voice, his skinny body, guys who'll never want him, Tokyo, Christmas…

Charlotte.

She's given him everything he needs, when no-else would or could. For nothing in return but love. She's nothing like him, but it's never kept her from understanding, or sympathising.

A click as her vape-pipe falls to the ground. She wraps her arms around him, squeezes him, holds his head. 'Darling! Oh Oscar, what's wrong? What's wrong, sweetheart?'

The sadness rises through him, has to lead somewhere. It's got to come to something.

But all that comes, after an age of noiseless shaking, is a sound as pitched and strangled as a shoe on a marble floor. He doesn't want to hear it again. But he does.

'Oscar…'

He buries his face in Charlotte's shoulder but it's no use. The tears roll into his mouth, saltwater.

His breathing slows.

His heart stops racing.

Charlotte is patting his back. 'I'll end it,' she says.

'No. No, I'm OK.'

'Really, it's not important.'

It's not important. What's gripped his head and shaken his body and woken him up is nothing to her. A thing that can be tossed aside.

She parts their bodies to look at his face, but the sight is too much for her. She pulls him back into her chest and holds him tight. Her delicate frame, bones like a sparrow's.

As if he'd ever leave her. Charlotte loves him. And she's not going anywhere. She's the one he needs.

13 DON'T KNOW YET SOMETHING

Not only did they make it to January without any snow, but now it's even got sunny. Maya suggested they meet at a teahouse near her work so she could pop in on her lunch break. They sit in mismatched chairs on a spacious wooden floor, Lukas' leg still managing to impeach on Oscar's boundaries. At least the leg is clothed. And rather than domination, there's an air of affection about it.

Maya says Bella looks tense, and starts to massage her shoulders. 'Get off me,' Bella says. 'I always look tense. It's my natural state, remember? *A Passage to India*.'

That prompts Lukas to tell them about his Indian client, who wants a website designed for a whack-sounding app. 'Woman is fussy as fuck,' he says. 'Like she thinks I can make her website 3D or something.'

Maya laughs. Floral-print dress against her smooth dark skin. Minimal — but expert — makeup. She's so at ease with her beauty, such a contrast to Bella with her thick-knit jumper.

'By the by, I might be joining you in the difficult-client club soon,' Bella says.

Maya's already gasping, happy. 'What?'

'Don't get excited, it's really nothing. But it's a definite improvement on my employment status.'

'You've got a job, though?'

Bella scoffs. 'Hardly. You know how Sammy has this startup… thing? I don't even know what the fuck he does, and I'm sure his clients don't know either. But anyway, part of it involves me proofreading his website and copy. And he said he'd pay me for it, but

I think he means in hummus. I was like, "Sammy, to correct your offensive abuse of commas would be all the reward I need." You seriously wouldn't guess his one and only language was English.'

'That's great though, B!'

'Yeah, it's...'

Oscar manages to speak. 'It's something.'

She pops a Murray Mint into her mouth, says, 'That's exactly what it is.' They know what the other's thinking. After a second she looks back to the others, inflates herself. 'They're all so boring, though, Sammy and his village of twats. All that dry, white-collar content and laddish guys who call their own conversations "banter". It gets on my tits.'

'A job's a job, though,' Lukas says. 'You do it 'cause you need to, not because you want to.'

Bella nods. 'So that just made me want to top myself.'

Maya laughs again, and squeezes Bella's shoulder. 'So proud of you! My little grammar Nazi.'

'Thanks, Mum. Speaking of whom, she's elated for me. I think I'll join the Greens to burst her bubble.'

Maya points at her. 'You can't be negative about this, yeah? I won't let you. If you decide you hate the job, then you'll be in a mood and hate the job. You don't need that energy.'

'You're right, M, I need positive vibes. Quick, bang a gong for me.'

'Such a cow,' Maya says, laughing despite herself.

Lukas watches Bella, those grey irises taking her in. There's a hint of sadness in his smile.

On the bus back to the centre, a girl with NHS specs and an oversized scarf is reading Charlotte's book. Tired of her mother, Bella hangs up on the woman mid-sentence, blaming signal problems. She leans against the back seat and spots the girl reading, nudges Oscar with a raised eyebrow. 'Have you read it yet?' she asks.

And it strikes Oscar that he hasn't, though the book's been out for months. It was the least he could've done, the knob. Bad son.

Bella shrugs, as if to say she doubts he's missing out. A row of trees moves past in the window behind her, their branches scratching the glass. 'Oh yeah! Is Charlotte seeing someone? I swear I saw a mention of something on a rag somewhere. I mean, it could've been bull—'

'She was, yeah.'

'Oh. So no more? You sly devil, why didn't you say?'

And from the way her expression changes, the rubbing of gel into her hands slowing down to a halt, he knows she's figured it out. Or, at least, a part of it. She holds his hand, and says nothing for the rest of the journey.

He knows what he has to do.

Tim replied to his text. He's accepted the invitation. They arrange to meet up at a deli in Borough, near the man's office.

All along the sunlit street, Oscar's stomach does kickflips, like those skater-boys in Mudchute. The low buildings, brown brick, feel as if they're closing in. Everything makes him jump. The sound of an iron gate closing as a guy, smart-casual, goes through the curved entrance of a yard. A pigeon taking off nearby. A cyclist. A truck.

Tim isn't in the deli yet, so Oscar gets out his smokes. The act does nothing to calm him. Maybe he should venture to the countryside for air. Or vape, like Charlotte.

She doesn't know he's here.

Christmas seemed to be the end of the road. After Tim got back from Nottingham, he never returned to the flat. Oscar stood alone on the balcony, smoking amongst the flora. For nights, for weeks. *Is Tim back in London yet?* he asked one morning at breakfast. And with an effort, Charlotte said, *I think so*. And that was that.

Maybe she told Tim about Oscar's feelings, and they decided it was better to part. They were always different, it was only ever going to be a brief-lived thing.

No. That isn't Charlotte's style. And Tim wouldn't have agreed to come if he knew the boy's feelings. Unless he harbours a Terry-like streak in him. Or that straight-guy need for an ego boost.

He sees him. Tim stands between two cars, about to cross the street, and spots Oscar outside the deli. His open smile says he hasn't got a clue. A van goes past, keeping the man at a distance for a little longer. Then a motorbike revs past, and Tim shakes his head, laughing, shy. He's only got a white shirt on beneath his coat, a scarf wound loosely around his neck.

The Eye is hidden in Oscar's pocket, a mere bump in his jeans.

When he finally makes it across the street, Tim puts his arms around Oscar in an easy manner and says it's good to see him. Mandarin and leather. 'Merry Christmas,' he adds. 'Happy New Year, all the big ones. Did I miss any?'

Oscar fights the urge to mention Valentine's Day around the corner. 'Nope.' The cigarette butt fizzles under his shoe.

'I'd usually be up for smoking one with you,' Tim says, 'but I'm flippin' famished. You ready to go in?'

He holds the door for Oscar to go inside. They sit at a little wooden table by the window, left in disarray by a ponytailed chick on a business call. Tim insists on treating Oscar, and orders panini and coffees for both of them. 'My dad would scoff at panini,' Tim says. 'To him it was a toastie, nothing else.'

For a while they only chat about Christmas, Tim's folks up in the Midlands. The man's annoyance with his nationalist brother-in-law, and relief at his unwaveringly socialist sister. The new music he's heard, the albums the new year will bring. 'How about you?' he says at one point. 'When can I expect the EP?' And he grins with half his mouth, letting Oscar know it was a harmless jab. He'll kick him up the arse, is what he meant, but he'll only do it gently.

Oscar's body comes close to relaxing, but he's kept from settling by a stab of cold air every time the door swings open. The subject is bound to come up, a pink elephant in the room. It sits on the table between them.

And then, it happens.

'How's Charlotte?' Tim asks. There's caution in his tone, a note of treading lightly.

'Yeah, she's alright.'

As the silence grows, Oscar's heart beats faster. The longer the pause, the harder it gets.

After a swallow, Tim picks up the thread. 'Did she tell you anything? About us, I mean.'

'Um… No, not really. I kind of guessed you broke up, but…'

Tim nods, chewing another mouthful. He gestures at his mouth, to show he can't speak while it's full. When he's finished, he says, 'It just couldn't work, right? We're so… opposite, really.'

'Yeah. Are you still working together, at least?'

'Oh yeah, it's not… Over-over. It was all very amicable.'

He goes back to his food. The mozzarella pulling itself from itself. The smell of the toasted ciabatta crust. Oscar still hasn't even tasted his, the nausea prevailing.

Despite Tim's talking about it, it's still not clear who broke up with whom. Or why. After all this effort, the planning, working up the courage to text and then finding the nerve to get here, to walk down this street with his mind and body a mess, he owes it to everyone to just come clean. He takes a breath, and goes for it. 'Have I ever told you about my friend Maya?'

It feels good to get it out. But his mouth is shivering.

'I don't think so, no.' Tim is surprised by the change of topic, and takes a sip of coffee.

'She's really into… spiritual stuff.'

'Oh,' Tim says, the half-smile exposing that chipped tooth.

'Yeah. And she was telling me about this thing called Constellations. They're a sort of, like, a way of proving that people understand each other without speaking. That we're all connected.'

'Hmm. I s'pose it's not that far-fetched.'

Oscar is taken aback. 'Really?'

'Well, yeah. We understand each other without needing to speak all the time. Body language, in't it. We're still animals when it boils down to it.'

Oscar had forgotten the Us and Os of Tim's accent. The way he says *in't it*. He has to go on. 'It's not just you, though. Like, sometimes they do it to show the feelings of people they've never even met. Like, I might bring an issue to the table and get other people to sort of act it out. Without them knowing about the issue beforehand.'

'Right…'

'It'll make sense in a minute.'

'Why, are you giving a demonstration?'

'… Are you up for it?'

Tim laughs, unnerved. 'You what?'

'Do you want to try it? I'll come up with a scenario, and we'll see if you can pick up on it through my thoughts.'

'This is very weird.' He stares as if a total stranger sat down in Oscar's place with no introduction. His coffee cup is not just an object he raises to his mouth, but a shield that keeps this nutter at a distance.

But this thing must be done. 'Please?'

With that, the funny look turns into a warm one. That of a put-upon dad with an offbeat kid who wants to play. 'Alright, then. Let's give it a bash.'

Relief and joy are almost enough to make Oscar forget the stakes. After all these months, it's finally happening. No chickening out. *I like you.*

'Should I close my eyes?' Tim says.

Maya never mentioned that.

'Do what you feel you should.'

'Excellent.' He keeps his eyes open.

'OK. At every stage, you have to tell me what you feel. Like, your gut instinct, whatever it is. Happy, mad, horny, whatever.'

Tim laughs. 'Horny?'

'Whatever,' he says, blushing. 'So, right now, how do you feel?'

Tim exhales. 'Very confused.'

'Good.' Oscar lets his gaze drift down. Tim's neck. The collar button undone.

'Um… Should I say something more?'

'When you feel it.'

As he tries to focus, Tim's eyes close. He's giving in, like he did to the old Greek broad.

The Swatch on his wrist. He and Oscar on the balcony together, smoking and talking.

Tim speaks. 'I actually feel a bit uncomfortable.'

Oscar's heart freezes. He can't lose the man's trust, not now. He should calm him, like you might a frightened horse. 'That's good.'

Tim looks pleased at this. Happy to have got the game.

The mixtape he made, on a loop in a darkened room. Oscar in bed, Jacques Brel's voice sinking into him. *Ne me quitte pas.*

'Huh,' Tim says. 'Now I feel a bit sad.'

Oscar's eyes sting. His teeth chatter in his closed mouth.

'That's really strange.'

Oscar's hand is on the Eye. Grips it through the fabric of his jeans.

I like you.

As loud in his head as if it had been spoken.

Tim opens his eyes. Whatever Oscar's expression is, he's reading it. He works through it as he blinks, as he takes in the boy's eyes, and hair, and lips. Until the half-smile disappears from his face. *I like you.* He heard it.

The silence between them lasts forever. Oscar has been stripped naked, and Tim approaches with caution. 'Correct me if I'm wrong…'

'You're not.'

He nods. 'How long have you felt this way?'

'A while.'

'Oscar—'

'I know.'

Tim is the only one who's ever had faith in him. To have a thought, a fire in his head. To be a worthwhile member of society. Tim is the first person he saw as a whole, when everyone else came in fragments. And as the man stares back at him, Oscar remembers to take him apart now, to store the details in his head. Those amber eyes in the sunlight, the flecks of red on the tips of his hair, the beauty spot above his lip, the stubble on his jaw, the chip in his tooth. Because London is a city of eight million faces, and he might never see this one again.

The scent of white fig greets him at the door. Charlotte's lit the candles along the sideboard as well as the table lamp by the sofa. She looks up from where she's sitting, Moleskine journal on her lap, pen at her mouth, to welcome him. There's food waiting for him in the kitchen, if he's hungry. Her smile grows warmer as he sits down next to her, mint and jasmine at her neck, and her hand curls around his. The moment is brief, ended with a peck on the cheek as he gets back up. Things are better left unsaid.

In the darkness of his bedroom, the blue light of the tape player flickers. The microphone Charlotte bought him sits on the mantlepiece, the laptop on the floor below. It isn't the time for those yet. When he gets his own place, he can set up a workspace, arrange them so it's all exactly as it should be. Months from now, maybe even weeks, this room will be a space he once inhabited. A patch of the city where he used to lay his head. Where he was once mothered, and loved, and blue and hopeless.

He puts the mixtape into the player. He recalls how Charlotte does it, pushes Play and Record at the same time. The tape clicks and rolls, a soft white noise washing over the tracks. Those songs Tim gave to him, now they'll be ghosts in the background of something else. Counterpoint. A memory.

I like you.

His voice is quiet as he sings. The tape player's mic will be too weak, barely able to pick him up. Logic tells him to lower his head to it, sing into the machine, but it feels better to sit on the bed, his body and mind at ease for the first in a long time, and sing whatever comes out. Let the recorder get what it gets.

It's time to look outwards. This is a revolt against himself, win or lose.

ABOUT THE AUTHOR

Polis Loizou is a co-founder of London's Off-Off-Off Broadway Company, which primarily performs his plays, and has had a series of successes since their first hit at the Brixton Fringe in 2009. His short stories have been featured in The Stockholm Review of Literature and Liars' League NYC, and he is a frequent contributor to Litro Magazine. Born and raised in Cyprus, Polis is currently based in South London. Disbanded Kingdom is his first published novel.